DragonRider

S. Rodman

Dark Angst Publishing

Copyright © 2023 by S. Rodman

All rights reserved.

No portion of this book may be reproduced in any form without written permission from the publisher or author, except as permitted by U.S. copyright law.

ISBN: 9798396316362

Cover design by S. Rodman.

ALL RIGHTS RESERVED: This literary work may not be reproduced or transmitted in any form or by any means, including electronic or photographic reproduction, in whole or in part, without express written permission.

All characters and events in this book are fictitious. Any resemblance to actual persons living or dead is strictly coincidental.

WARNING: The unauthorized reproduction or distribution of this copyrighted work is illegal. Criminal copyright infringement, including infringement without monetary gain, is investigated by the FBI and is punishable by up to 5 years in federal prison and a fine of $250,000.

Contents

Dubious Consent

Concern that a main character is planning suicide

Contents

Dedication	VI
Foreword	VII
1. Chapter 1	1
2. Chapter 2	13
3. Chapter 3	23
4. Chapter 4	29
5. Chapter 5	37
6. Chapter 6	47
7. Chapter 7	53
8. Chapter 8	65
9. Chapter 9	71
10. Chapter 10	77
11. Chapter 11	87
12. Chapter 12	93

13.	Chapter 13	99
14.	Chapter 14	105
15.	Chapter 15	113
16.	Chapter 16	125
17.	Chapter 17	141
18.	Chapter 18	147
19.	Chapter 19	157
20.	Chapter 20	163
21.	Chapter 21	171
22.	Chapter 22	179
23.	Chapter 23	191
24.	Chapter 24	199
25.	Chapter 25	205
26.	Chapter 26	211
27.	Chapter 27	217
28.	Chapter 28	223
29.	Chapter 29	231
30.	Chapter 30	237
31.	Chapter 31	245
32.	Chapter 32	251

33. Chapter 33	259
Acknowledgments	265
Thank You	267
Books By S. Rodman	269

Jesse H Reign
You are a wonderful friend
A terrible influence
& incredibly inspiring.
Never change.

Author's note

This book is written in British English. I apologise for the confusion. I normally write in American English, even though I'm British and a few of my books are set in the UK.

This book wouldn't let me.

Chapter One

I hate Wales. It's official. If I ever gain super powers, I'm blasting it to oblivion. The roads are tiny and winding. There are far too many mountains and zero phone signal, so my map app isn't working and now I'm hopelessly lost, very late, and my piece of shit car is about to overheat and die on me and there isn't even anywhere to pull over and cry.

I can't call for directions or to apologise for running late. Everything has turned into an absolute nightmare.

All I wanted to do was drive to Caernyddyn Castle, set some wards and sigils, get paid and leave. But no, this damn country is determined to destroy me. I mean, it shouldn't be this blasted hard to find a castle. It's a frigging *castle!*

Even if I admit defeat, I'm not sure I can find my way back to the main road. I'm cursed to drive around the backwaters of Wales for the rest of eternity, never to find my way out. Never to return home to England.

Suddenly, up ahead I see a tractor on the side of the road. The farmer is fiddling with a gate. Either shutting it or opening it, I can't tell and I don't care.

I stop in the middle of the road, but it's not like I have seen another vehicle for twenty minutes. If something does come along, they will just have to bloody well wait.

The farmer is already looking at me, so I wind down my window and put on my brightest smile.

"Hi! I'm looking for ..." Shit I have no idea how to pronounce Caernyddyn. "Care-nid-din Castle," I attempt.

The farmer looks at me like I'm crazy. His weather-worn face is scrunched up in bewilderment. Did I really mangle it that badly?

I try again, "Care-nye-din?"

"Car-nith-in," says the farmer, slowly and carefully. As if I am a small child.

I blink. Is he talking about the right place? I don't know how he got those sounds from the spelling I've seen. It would just be my luck to get directions to entirely the wrong place.

"Yeah?" I say uselessly. I just have to hope for the best.

"Keep going for about a mile and then take the next left."

Okay, that doesn't sound too bad. Even I can follow directions that simple.

"Thank you so much!" I beam.

The farmer smiles back at me, "No problem."

I give him a little wave and then set off. Oh, my god. I just waved at him. What the hell is wrong with me? Do I think I'm the queen or something? Okay, deep breath. It is a little cringe, but look on the bright side. He can tell his friends about the crazy English person who asked for directions and acted like a complete nutcase. I might have just made his day.

The road ambles around a corner and opens up to a stunning vista. It's all green fields and trees as far as the eye can see. A sparkling river snakes its way through the bottom of the valley. Wow. Okay, I'll admit that when you aren't panicking and lost, Wales is beautiful. Maybe I'll come back for a holiday.

If I can ever afford one. My stomach twists in all-too familiar knots. Money is a constant stress. But things are looking up. These people reached out to hire me. If I do a good job, they might recommend me to others. My freelance mage business might actually start going somewhere. Who knows, maybe my luck might be about to turn. Stranger things have happened.

My derisive snort echoes around the empty car. Yeah right. Who I'm I kidding. My luck has been shit for the first twenty-three years of my life. It has no reason to change now.

I see a left turn and take it cautiously. The farmer did say the first left turn, didn't he? Or did he mean the first left turn after driving a mile? For fuck's sake. I have no idea. I think I have driven about a mile anyway, so let's hope for the best.

Suddenly, an enormous castle comes into view, and I shriek in delight. Thank heavens. Now just to hope that it's the right castle, this is Wales after all. It's not known for its shortage of castles.

I turn into a short driveway that opens into a wide expanse of beige coloured gravel. Around twenty cars are strewn around in no particular order that I can see, so I tuck mine into a corner that seems out of the way and like it won't block anyone in. It's the best I can do.

I scramble out because I'm super late. The castle looks imposing. From here, I can mostly just see a tall windowless wall of grey stone. There is a huge archway in the middle, so I guess the door is through there. Do castles have doorbells? I guess I'm about to find out.

Why do the people who live here want magical wards and sigils protecting them? The question still rattles around my head even though I decided to ignore it ages ago, because, hello, I'm getting paid, so who cares?

But the Venn diagram of people who know about the paranormal, need protection, but can't do it themselves, is tiny. Probably non-existent. When I set up my freelance mage services on the dark web, I had expected to be hired for boring, monotonous work no one else wanted to do.

I let out a little snort laugh. My business model is clearly deeply flawed. Starting with the *expected to be hired* bit.

My thoughts come to a shuddering halt. Someone is striding out of the archway, looking like they are heading straight for me. My body is going crazy. I freeze as if my feet have taken root in the crunchy gravel. Tingling goosebumps have erupted over every inch of my skin. My stomach is role playing as a washing machine and my lungs have forgotten to breathe.

Who is this guy?

I've never had such a visceral reaction to another person. What is going on?

He is tall and slender. Pale hair the colour of starlight falls to his shoulders. Black leather trousers fit his legs like a second skin. He is wearing boots and my brain can't interpret the top he is wearing but it's black leather too. I can't place his style. It's not quite 'hot goth boy'. Nor is it 'biker'. Even though something about all that leather screams practical rather than style.

He is right next to me now and I have to tilt my head to look up at him. My gaze lingers on his gorgeous cheekbones before reaching his eyes. The moment our eyes meet. I physically jolt, as if I have been electrocuted. There is so much to see in his eyes. Power, pain, magic and a multitude of other things I cannot begin to name.

"Kirby Taylor?" he asks.

I nod. For some reason, I'm entirely too tongue-tied to say a single word. He carries authority with him, the type I've only ever felt before from much older men. He has to be mid to late twenties at the most, yet something about him makes it perfectly clear that he is used to giving orders and being obeyed.

"You're late," he says and I watch in horror as a sneer crosses his face.

I don't want him to sneer at me. I want him to like me. No, I need him to like me. The feeling is as intense as it is unsettling. I just met the guy, what on earth has come over me? I'm not normally like this.

"Sorry, I had trouble finding it," I babble helplessly.

One perfect eyebrow raises. "It's a castle."

There is so much scorn and derision in his voice that I could probably bottle it and use it in a hex. The force of it makes me wither.

"Come!" he says imperiously, as he turns on his heels and starts striding back towards the castle.

I trot after him like a well-trained dog. As if his command bypassed the conscious part of my mind and went straight to my nervous system. What the hell?

"Who *are* you?"

His shoulders stiffen but he doesn't slow his stride. Oh my god, I can't believe I asked my question out loud and in such a tone of bewildered exasperation.

"Mordecai Mordred."

My eyebrows rise. "That's quite a name."

His pace quickens, but he gives no other sign that he has heard me. Which is probably a good thing. My tone was quite mocking. Jesus, this guy has a strange effect on me, including bringing out my worst side.

We walk out into a wide courtyard paved with flagstones and surrounded by impressive castle walls. This place is stunning. He stops suddenly and whirls to face me and I nearly walk into him.

"You are good at portals?" he asks.

I blink at him in confusion. None of the emails I received when being hired mentioned anything about portals. Though I do boast about my ability on my website.

"Yes?" I say, somehow managing to make it sound like a question.

"Show me," he orders.

I stare at him in confusion. Portals take a huge amount of magic, they are incredibly draining. If I create one, I'll be too depleted to do the work they hired me for. Nevermind that one does not simply go around creating portals willy-nilly. They are not frivolous things. They are for emergencies and very serious matters. Otherwise I would have just portaled here from my shitty flat and not lost hours of my life driving around Wales.

He seriously wants me to create one? And just to show him? Show him what? That I can do magic? There are easier and better ways to test that. Besides, can he not sense my magic? I can sure as hell sense his. Rolling off of him in potent waves.

"Do it!" he snaps as he crosses his arms.

There is a slight Welsh lilt to his voice, and it's extremely enticing. He is the most distracting man I have ever had the misfortune to meet. But I need to concentrate. I need to prove to him that I'm not some helpless, gormless worm. I am a very competent mage, thank you very much. And he wants me to open a portal.

"To anywhere in particular?" I ask.

"No."

Well, fuck him then. I close my eyes, concentrate on the spell and with only three hand gestures open up a portal to the north pole, aiming it so the arctic wind blasts right at him.

He doesn't so much as flinch. He merely shuts my portal down with a lazy hand gesture, as if he is casually swatting a fly.

"Can you do it with your eyes open?"

Glaring right into his condescending face I open a portal to the Sahara desert. This time a blast of scorching air blows orange sand into his perfect hair.

He frowns, and closes my portal with a click of his fingers.

Then he opens one up, right by my toes. A large one. Humid Amazonian air hits me right in my face. A mosquito buzzes out and a deadly looking snake looks far too interested in slithering over.

"Close it."

I can't do it with a snap of my fingers or as if I'm swatting a fly. But I manage it with four rapid hand gestures.

Eddies of arctic, desert and jungle air swirl for a moment in the courtyard, before dissipating and returning the atmosphere around us to normal Welsh summer air.

We glare at each but I think I see a flash of respect in his eyes and I hate how much I crave more of it.

"You'll do. I suppose."

I honestly don't know if I am offended or flattered by that. He makes me so confused.

"Do for what?" I hear myself ask.

Something flashes in his eyes and he sighs heavily, as if the weight of the entire world is on his shoulders. Completely over reacting to being asked a simple question.

"This is a Dragonrider fortress. An unbonded dragon has decided to take a rider. The ceremony requires thirteen young unbonded mages to present to the dragon. Between all the rider families we could only rustle up twelve. So you are here to make up the numbers."

I feel my jaw drop open. What the hell? I don't get the joke. What is going on? I'm so confused. Dragons? There is no such thing as dragons. They are one of the few mythical creatures that don't actually exist.

Mordecai stares at me as I gulp like a fish out of water. Then he huffs.

"Don't worry about it. You just need to stand on the battlement and look pretty. Ri is not going to choose you.

After the ceremony, I'll have to go into your vile little mind and wipe your memories. By Monday, you'll be back home thinking you spent a wet weekend camping in Wales."

I stare at him. I'm incredulous. Outraged. Insulted. Vile little mind? How dare he? But none of my emotions are translating into words.

He glares at me impatiently, waiting for me to speak. But I really can't. After a moment, he makes a noise of pure derision.

"I haven't got time for this. Stay there. I'll send Harlen to look after you."

He turns on his heels and strides away. Damn that bastard is fast. I stare at his rapidly disappearing back and still can't say anything. Dragons? Is he insane as well as ludicrously and infuriatingly hot? With a temperament like that, he deserves to be hideously ugly. There is no justice in the world.

I'm standing alone in a courtyard in a castle in Wales. The one inhabitant I have met is a rude, obnoxious weirdo. I should definitely flee. Run back to my car and never look back. But I know myself well enough to know that I won't. I'm curious now. And yes, curiosity killed the cat but oh well, I'm pretty sure unresolved curiosity would drive me completely insane. So I'm just going to stand here like a pleb and wait for this Harlen. Because what if Mordecai is not nuts? What if dragons are real?

A shiver dances along my spine. Excitement. Trepidation. And the feeling that my entire life might be about to change.

Chapter Two

Anxiety is really getting its claws into me. Standing here on my own, twiddling my thumbs feels so damn awkward. Maybe I should leave.

Footsteps sound behind me, and I whirl to face them. An audible gasp escapes me, but thankfully I think he is too far away to hear it. Is everyone in this place insanely good looking? Is it something in the water?

This guy is tall, though not as tall as Mordecai. He is broader too, filled out with muscles that his tight tee shirt does nothing to hide. His skin is golden, either a really good tan or Mediterranean ancestry, I can't tell. He has a mop of dark curls and warm brown eyes. And a bright smile.

He closes the distance between us in no time and holds out his hand. Numbly I offer my own and am soon engulfed in a vigorous handshake. His hand is larger than mine, calloused and chucking out some fierce heat. I don't want to let it go.

"Hi!" he says brightly. "I'm Harlen." He sounds English, like me.

"Kirby." Some part of my brain that is still functioning, manages to reply.

"Nice to meet you!" he grins.

I stare at him blankly. He is like an exuberant force of nature. Blowing me away with his sheer presence. It's every bit as intense as Mordecai's, but so very different. Harlen is sunshine, and Mordecai is pale moonlight.

"So Cai dropped the dragon bomb on you and then scarpered?" says Harlen with a wry grin.

I blink for a moment before stuttering out, "Yeah." My gaze nervously flicks to where Mordecai stormed off, as if I think he is going to come striding back in fury.

Harlen follows my gaze and then clasps my shoulder.

"Don't worry about Cai, he is a prickly bastard, but he is adorable once you get to know him."

I can't stop the incredulous and disbelieving look that is spreading across my face. Mordecai and adorable are not things that go together, in any universe. Harlen gives a hearty laugh. I guess he is not offended that I don't believe him, which is a relief I suppose. But then - wait a minute. Harlen said 'Dragon bomb' and I completely ignored it to fixate on Mordecai. Talk about messed up priorities.

"Dragons!" I exclaim suddenly. "You think dragons are real too?"

It's not just Mordecai who is deluded? Maybe it's one of those shared delusions? I've heard of those. They are rare and bizarre but still make a hell of a lot more sense than Dragons existing but no one in the paranormal community knowing about them. Maybe there really is something in the water here, something that makes people incredibly hot and completely insane?

Harlen grins again. "You'll be meeting one soon enough. There is just about enough time for a tour of the castle first."

I shake my head. "Fuck the castle! Explain this dragon shit to me!"

My hands smack over my mouth in horror. What on earth is wrong with me? Why am I being so rude?

"I'm sorry," I mumble through my hands.

"As fiery as your hair," says Harlen with a truly filthy wink that flips my stomach over.

Oh hells. Now I'm annoyed at the red head joke and completely bamboozled by his apparent flirting. He is way too hot to be flirting with me. He is easily a ten and I scrape a four on a good day. That knowledge does nothing to dampen my libido. It registered the flirtatious wink and is now all sorts of excited. Swooning in his arms is a real possibility. Fuck.

"Tell me about dragons," I plead with gritted teeth. I need the distraction before I embarrass myself even more than I already have.

Harlen's expression sobers. "Shall we go sit down somewhere? It's going to be a lot to take in."

I shake my head. "Just tell me, please."

"Okay then," says Harlen. "So, dragons are real. There are families of dragon riders who bond with them, and we ride them at night to stop interdimensional beings attacking Earth."

I really should have taken that seat.

"I beg your pardon?"

Okay, at least my shock is making me polite now, instead of rude. That's an improvement.

Harlen gives me a truly scrutinising look. "How about we find a seat and a cup of tea?" He seems worried. As if he thinks I might be about to faint.

"Yes, alright," I mutter, since I do feel a little lightheaded.

He takes my arm and starts guiding me to one of the doors. Normally I hate being touched, nevermind being led around like a puppy, but for some reason this doesn't bother me at all. It actually feels nice. Comforting. Reassuring.

Before I really know what is happening, Harlen takes me to a surprisingly normal looking living room, sits me on a very comfortable sofa and shoves a cup of sweet milky tea into my shaking hands.

"Interdimensional beings?" I whisper after taking a sip.

"Ah yes. Think of them as demons or aliens. Whichever works for you. We call them tylwyth."

I stare at him in complete bewilderment for a few heartbeats. "Demons or aliens, but you call them Welsh fairies?"

Harlen laughs. "It's all the same thing. Beings from somewhere else, not of this realm."

A shudder rushes through me. "Why are you fighting them?"

"They open small portals high up in the sky, only big enough for one tylwyth to pass through. They try to reach the ground, especially specific places like stone circles and the pyramids. We suspect once there, they can use devices to open up a huge portal and let the mother ship or demon horde through, depending on how you are choosing to think of it."

"You suspect?"

I watch mesmerised as a truly shit-eating grin spreads across Harlen's face. His teeth are white and gleaming. Perfect just like the rest of him.

"Suspect, because in hundreds of years we've never let a single bastard make it."

I'm back to staring. But it seems Harlen is on a roll now and doesn't need me to say anything.

"Dragons enable us to reach the portals. Riders close the portals and both of us together chase the bastards down the sky, eating, incinerating, decapitating or impaling, whatever works. Just as long as they don't reach earth alive."

The only thing I can do is blink. My mind has shut down access to every other part of my body. I guess it needs every brain cell it can muster to try to process what I just heard. The words Harlen said just don't make sense. Maybe I'm the crazy one? Maybe this is all a hallucination? Maybe I drove around for too long in my shitty car and now have, I don't know, carbon monoxide poisoning or something? Or I spun off the road and crashed down the mountain and this is all just a coma dream.

My gaze rakes over Harlen's perfect body. Well, I give my imagination ten out of ten for conjuring hot guys. Mordecai was complete wet dream material too. Why is my subconscious so horny? It hasn't been that long since I got laid. I mean two years is nothing, right? Okay, okay, as soon as I wake up, I'm going to hunt down some action. Anything to stop my mind from pulling an intervention like this again.

I wince as I catch up with my train of thought. Mordecai and Harlen aren't real? Just figments of my imagination? That hurts. A lot. It feels like grief and makes my chest tight. I want them to be real. I want dragons to be real.

"Are you alright?" asks Harlen.

"No, not really," I confess.

He gives me a soft smile and places a warm hand on my knee. The feel of his touch sets my entire body tingling.

"Don't worry, it's very likely Ri won't choose you and Cai will erase your memories. You only have to deal with this for a couple of hours."

I glare at Harlen. Why is everyone so convinced that I won't be chosen? Do I come across as unworthy? I'm a damn good mage and I'd make a magnificent dragon rider, thank you very much!

"I don't want my memories erased," is all I say. I really need to work on my assertiveness.

Harlen's smile turns sympathetic. "It won't hurt."

That's really not the point. I don't want anyone rummaging in my mind, tampering with things. The whole idea feels squicky and far too intimate.

"Will I remember you?"

I can't believe I just said that. I stare at Harlen and fight to keep the horror off my face. Play it cool, like a cat. Pretend that I meant to say that and I'm totally fine with it.

"I'm afraid not," he says gently, but with a gleam in his eyes.

He likes that I want to remember him. I guess it is an ego boost. I'd definitely be flattered. Thing is, is he actually interested in me, or does he merely love the idea of anyone not wanting to forget him?

"How long is your hair?" he asks suddenly.

My hand flies up to my messy man bun and I feel a flush spread across my cheeks. "Why?"

"I've been trying to imagine it loose, and it's driving me crazy," he says with a very naughty smirk.

I swallow dryly as my heart races in my chest. "Stupidly long."

He tilts his head. "Is it a religious thing?"

"No! Well, only accidentally. I heard the story of Samson and Delilah when I was young and refused to have my hair cut and it just sort of stuck. Then my ex was always on about me cutting it and it was the only thing I ever stood up to him on, so I'm keeping it now. As a reminder."

Oh. My. God. Why did I just say all that? What the hell is wrong with me? Way to kill a mood. The correct response would have been to give him a sultry look and say something like, 'why don't we go somewhere private so I can show you how long it is?'

This is why I've not been laid for two years. Nothing to do with trauma from my ex. Just my complete and utter inability to flirt.

"Your ex sounds like an asshole," says Harlen kindly.

Yep, mood well and truly ruined. His interest has been replaced with pity. Just fucking great. I can feel the disappointment rolling in my belly. A physical manifestation of my feelings of failure.

I take a deep breath and try to calm down. It's fine. If the flirting had gone well, the sex would have been a disaster. So it's all good. I've never had a random hookup and I'm terrible in bed, so this humiliation is far better than getting that far, only to have Harlen disappointed in me.

The fantasy of engaging in casual sex is far more enticing than the real thing would ever be.

"Ready to meet a dragon?" asks Harlen.

I nearly spit out my tea. "What, right now?"

"It's time for the ceremony," he grins.

Well, fuck me.

Chapter Three

It's windy up here on the battlement. It's supposed to be summer, but it is Wales and I'm only wearing a tee shirt. My body is shivering but I'm not paying it much attention. I'm too intrigued with what is happening. I'm standing on a castle wall, with twelve other young mages. We are facing an inner courtyard that has the frigging side of a mountain as one of its walls. Apparently there is an enormous cave mouth hidden by a cloaking spell and any minute now, a dragon is going to stroll out of the mountain.

If this is a hoax or a prank, it's very elaborate and I have no idea why anyone would go to so much effort. It's not like I have any friends. There is no one to be amused by fooling me. In my experience, nobody finds tricking strangers any fun at all. But, if I'm in a coma dream or hallucination, it's really bloody vivid.

Whatever the hell is going on, I really, really want to see what happens next. I'm staring at the mountain as if I can will it to open up and reveal its secrets. I can't help but notice that they have positioned me last. The furthest from the alleged cave entrance. I know one thing is definitely true, Dragonriders are assholes.

Harlen said the only reason he didn't think the dragon would pick me is because I'm not from a rider family, it's not in my blood. As if that makes it any better. It just makes them snobby assholes or racist ones.

Whatever. It's frustrating but there is not a lot I can do about it. If dragons are real, I'd love to be picked, because, hello? *Dragons.* It would also be immensely satisfying to see the look on these Dragonriders faces. Sadly, I have absolutely no idea how to get a dragon to pick me to be its rider. So wiping those smirks of their smug faces is going to have to remain a fun little fantasy. If this whole situation isn't already one.

I sigh in exasperation at my spiralling thoughts and wrap my arms around myself in an effort to keep warm. *Come on, dragon. Let's get this over with.* I send the thought out lazily but then jolt in surprise. I swear I just felt something. A feather soft brush against my mind. Like a whisper just too quiet for me to hear. I really am losing the plot.

As if to confirm my lack of sanity, the mountain begins to shimmer, and a dragon strides out. An actual real life dragon. Smaller than I pictured, it's around the size of an elephant. Its scales are ink black yet they glimmer iridescent in the sunlight. Some of the scales are gilded with gold along the edges.

The dragon's wings are curled neatly along its back. There are some spikes along its face, but the dragon doesn't look monstrous or reptilian. It looks beautiful. Magical. Mythical. Wise. It is easily the most stunning being I have ever seen.

It swivels its head and one dazzling amber eye seems to regard me for a moment. My heart thuds loudly, but the magnificent being turns its attention to the first mage. With us standing on the battlement wall, which isn't actually that tall, and the dragon standing on the courtyard floor, its head is level with us. Though he does have to stretch his long neck up to reach.

I watch, utterly transfixed as he sniffs the first mage. Then he regally moves onto the second one. Does that mean the first one hasn't been chosen, or that he is going to sniff us all before he chooses? I hope it's the latter, because it will be an honour to get that close to him, to feel his breath on my skin. It would be awe-inspiring.

I simply have to find a way of keeping my memories of this. I need to somehow figure out how to make a magical strongbox in my mind. This is far too precious to lose. I want to cherish it forever.

As I ponder the magical problem, the dragon slowly makes his way down the line of mages. Sniffing them all carefully as he goes. I wonder what I smell like? Old car and cheap deodorant, probably. I wish I'd known about any of this. I'd have brought sage or sandalwood or perhaps even catnip. There is something feline in the way the dragon moves, and in his expression. It might just be that he knows he is superior. But I still would love to try catnip. It would definitely be worth a go.

Eventually he reaches me and I'm vibrating with excitement. Up close he is truly gorgeous. He snuffles me with gentle huffs of warm air that smell of spice.

"May I touch you?" I breathe in awe.

The dragon regards me for a moment then gracefully ducks his head in a clear nod. I reach out and run a hand reverently over the spiny ridge above his eye. He feels warm to the touch and oh so smooth. My hand is tingling with the magic he exudes. He is incredible.

Harlen mentioned that the dragon's name was Ri. It really suits him. Somehow the one syllable manages to be both regal and mysterious.

"Pleased to meet you, Ri. I'm Kirby."

Nobody bothered to tell me how intelligent dragons are. For all I know, they could be like enormous dogs. But when he first walked out, I looked into Ri's brilliant amber eyes, and I know a highly intelligent sentient being when I see one.

Ri huffs again and gently bats his head against me, for all the world like a huge cat. I laugh and stroke him with both hands. For his size, he is incredibly gentle.

"Congratulations!" says Harlen, suddenly right beside me.

I turn to him and blink in confusion. Harlen gives me a beaming, shit-eating grin. I don't understand what he is so happy about. He gets to see dragons all the time, the lucky bastard.

"Ri has chosen you."

I turn back to the dragon. "You have?" I exclaim in astonishment.

Ri does another one of his graceful head bobs that look like a nod and then I shriek in delight and jump up and down on the spot. I think I'm babbling a string of thank you's over and over again but I'm not really sure. I'm far too giddy with excitement.

This is hands down, without doubt, the happiest and best day of my life.

Chapter Four

This study or office or whatever it is, is lovely. Ornate dark wood bookshelves line the walls and are practically groaning with the weight of all the beautiful books they are stuffed full of. The large desk looks antique and the Persian rug is a vibrant blue that I've never seen captured in a carpet before. Everything is illuminated by the sweeping lead-lined windows.

Harlen had to drag me away from Ri to here, but now I'm not even sure I mind. Maybe I should ask if that offer of a tour of the castle still stands. If this is a glimpse of what it looks like, I'd be thrilled to see more.

Though right now, I'd still prefer to spend more time with Ri. He is amazing and I want to get to know him. And I just want to absorb every detail, along with the undeniable reality of him, because even now, ten minutes away from the dragon, I can feel the doubt starting to creep in. I'm starting to wonder if being chosen really did happen.

Mordecai strides in and takes the seat behind the desk. He glares at me with ice-blue eyes. I stare at him in surprise. Not only has he startled me from my thoughts, I wasn't expecting him at all. This is his office? Damn.

"Flight Commander," says Harlen and I can hear a trace of mockery in his tone.

Mordecai scowls at him before turning his withering attention to me. It's so hard not to wilt before him, but I do have a backbone, goddamn it!

"How did you trick Ri into choosing you?" he snaps.

What the hell? How dare he? He has to be the rudest most pompous ass alive. What the fuck is his problem with me?

"I didn't do anything!" I protest.

Oh shit. That sounded so whiny and petulant when it was meant to sound confident and indignant. This is awful. I need to fix it. I can do this. Taking comfort from Harlen's presence beside me, I take a deep breath and try again.

"How could I do anything? I knew nothing about dragons until this morning. How would I know how to trick one?"

There, that was much better. I sounded calm and reasonable with just enough of a slightly condescending tone to piss Mordecai off. I can almost feel Harlen's amusement.

Mordecai's eyes narrow, and he leans back in his chair before steepling his long fingers. The whole look is giving off strong supervillain vibes. It should be funny, but the bastard can pull it off and I'm actually genuinely intimidated.

"You are going to have to think of something convincing to tell your parents about why you are suddenly living in a castle in Wales."

Parents? I'm twenty-three years old for flip's sake. I'm not a child.

"I don't have any parents," I snap.

"Why not?" he bites back.

"Because they're dead, dipshit!" I all but yell.

One perfect eyebrow raises. "Well, that makes things easier."

My jaw drops open. No apology? No, 'I'm sorry for your loss'? It is...strangely refreshing. I blink at him in bewilderment. I usually hate the dead parents conversation. People get all awkward and flustered which makes me all flummoxed and uncomfortable. I actually like this version of it. No fuss. No nonsense.

"Girlfriend?" he asks.

I shake my head. "It would be a boyfriend, but no I don't have one."

Something flashes across Mordecai's eyes and his expression shifts ever so slightly. That can't have been interest? He can't be pleased that I'm gay. Harlen is clearly into men, so what are the chances that the two hottest guys I have ever seen, both swing my way? Not that it changes anything. They are both stupendously out of my league. And Mordecai is a horrid jerk anyway. But at least I will not be living with homophobes.

"Good. What about friends, your job?"

Great, I can feel my cheeks heating up. Being pale skinned is the absolute worst. I have no wish to display my every emotion.

"A few casual acquaintances. I'll just tell them I got a job in Wales. And I'm self-employed."

Mordecai just nods thoughtfully. He doesn't seem amused by my sad little life and my lack of friends. It doesn't look like he is going to mock me for it. He is a confusing son of a bitch.

But then again, I'm confusing too. I've met a dragon for all of ten minutes and I'm willing to give up my entire life, with no hesitation. Granted, it's not much of a life, but I swear it's still an odd reaction. But then, judging by Mordecai's behaviour, it is certainly the expected one. I can't even begin to imagine his face if I declined.

Mordecai stares at me intently and then huffs in displeasure.

"Perhaps this won't be quite such a disaster," he says grudgingly.

The look in his eyes says very clearly that he still thinks this is going to be a disaster, because he thinks I am a disaster. The man only just met me and he has written me off as a loser. As much as I wish I didn't care, his judgement hurts.

"Cai," says Harlen softly, and it sounds like more than an admonishment, it sounds like a warning.

Mordecai's intense gaze flicks to Harlen and they battle something out until Mordecai looks away first and shifts his position in his chair. When he looks at me again, his expression is softer.

"We'll do the binding ceremony tonight and you'll start intensive training tomorrow." His tone is still curt, but he is no longer looking at me as if I'm something disgusting he found on his shoe.

I nod at him but I'm distracted by what just happened between the two men. I swear Mordecai is in charge here, the office, his attitude, the way Harlen addressed him by his rank or title or whatever it is, all gives that impression. Yet he definitely just seemed to defer to Harlen. I'm so confused.

"Harlen can find you a room and give you the tour."

"Yes, Flight Commander," says Harlen and the mockery is super clear this time.

I wince, but Mordecai just glowers at him and says nothing. Surely that counts as insubordination? Why is he letting Harlen get away with it? I don't get the impression that they are good friends and therefore just rile each other all the time. In fact, it feels like there is a fair bit of animosity between them. Does Harlen think he should be in charge?

Whatever the hell is going on, it's going to be a lot to untangle. And that's before you add in dragons and nightly battles with interdimensional beings. What the hell have I got myself into?

Harlen leads me out of the study. As soon as we are in the hallway, he turns to me.

"Don't mind Cai. He is like that to everyone. Don't take it personally."

I give him a disbelieving look. "So when is he adorable?"

Harlen laughs. A deep rich musical laugh, full of glee. He is acting like the fact I recall his words from a few hours ago is deeply hilarious.

He gives me a playful shove with his elbow. "You'll see," he says mysteriously.

I hate how intrigued I am. I should stay well away from Mordecai, well as much as I can, given he is a flight commander, whatever that means. I shouldn't want to unravel his puzzle pieces and try to see what is under his prickly exterior. But I do. Almost as much as I want to see this new home of mine and be bonded to Ri. My priorities are certainly strange.

"Going to show me this castle then?" I ask Harlen.

He gives me a grin and an elaborate, sweeping bow. His head being level with my waist, gives my body all sorts of wrong ideas, even though he is only down there for a second.

"Right this way, kind sir," he says.

I can't help but grin back. At least Harlen is nice. And that is far more reassuring than it should be. I thought I'd learnt that lesson the hard way and long ago. People can't be trusted. I wonder if dragons can be?

Chapter Five

"It's a bit Game of Thrones in here, isn't it?" I say.

Harlen laughs, and the sound echoes around the cavernous underground chamber. Mordecai ignores me, as if he didn't hear me speak at all. He just continues to stride ahead of me, holding his flaming torch up high. In the flickering shadows and eerie setting, he looks even more alluring. All haughty, mysterious and magical. Damn him.

"We were here long before George. R. R. Martin," says Harlen. "So he is copying us, not the other way around."

"Is he copying you?" I ask in surprise. Has the author been here? It would certainly explain a lot.

"No!" snaps Mordecai. "Only Dragonriders know about Dragonriders. So it has always been and so it will always be."

Harlen drops back so he can pull a face without Mordecai seeing. Even in the dim light, the sparkle of merriment in his dark eyes is clear to see. It's hard to stifle my laugh.

I'm glad Mordecai truly is sounding like a pompous ass and it's not just me being over sensitive.

But as we walk deeper into the chamber the gravity of the situation starts to sink in. Our feet rustle over ancient flagstones. Our shadows dance along the impressive walls. I can feel the weight of aeons. I can taste the passage of time on my tongue. The stars have spun across the night sky a thousand times and shifted positions since this chamber was built. To the stone I am surrounded by, my life is as fleeting as a raindrop.

Greater people than I built this place. Greater people than me will come after. I'm merely taking up my place in the weave of time. A placeholder.

A Dragonrider. Protecting Earth.

I barely understand what it entails, as I only have Harlen's brief explanation to go on, but it's enough to understand the magnitude of the role. The importance of it.

A wave of dizziness washes over me. Am I up to the task? The sheer responsibility is overwhelming. Ri is wonderful, but will I be any good as a rider? Am I good enough? Just because I want to do it, doesn't mean I should.

I'm excited to see Ri again, and complete whatever ritual officially binds us, but am I doing the right thing? Hanging out with a dragon is one thing, flying around on one and battling invaders and closing portals is quite another. It sounds like an exhilarating life. One of meaning. One I would be honoured to lead. But my desires do not make me worthy.

A warm hand envelopes mine and gives me a reassuring squeeze.

"There is no need to be nervous," whispers Harlen.

Shit. Am I that easy to read? I don't mind Harlen knowing I'm scared, but I want to impress Mordecai. Fuck knows why. I shouldn't care about his opinion of me. But I do. I'm yearning for his respect like a flower seeking the sun. It's absurd but I'm powerless before it.

We've reached a large stone altar. Mordecai and Harlen place their flaming torches in sconces set into pillars near the ends of the raised altar. I can't see Ri or any dragons, but the spicy smell that I have already come to associate with the magnificent beings, is everywhere.

"You need to lie on the altar," says Mordecai.

"Naked," adds Harlen.

I stare at him in horror, and he bursts into laughter, doubling up with the force of it. It takes my startled mind a moment to fully process that he was joking and he finds my horrified expression greatly amusing.

"Child," mutters Mordecai disapprovingly, and for once I actually agree with the moody bastard.

"Sorry!" wheezes Harlen, still not able to stand up properly.

He doesn't sound the least bit sorry to me. And it hurts. It's unsettling. He probably meant well, but what if he didn't? What if he had played it out for longer and I had actually stripped? What if he is not as nice as he seems? My ex totally fooled me into thinking he was a good person. Clearly my character judgement skills suck big time.

"Wing Commander Harlen Bracebridge. Your behaviour is inappropriate." Mordecai's voice is cold and deadly serious.

Harlen winces and straightens, nearly to attention. "Apologies, Flight Commander."

At least he sounds genuinely contrite now. Mordecai nods and I can tell the matter is dropped. I flash him a smile of thanks and am surprised by the tiny smile I get in return. These men are so confusing. And they have so much responsibility, as evidenced by the way they both just effortlessly jumped into their formal roles. They aren't much older than me and it's disconcerting. I always thought I was mature for my age, but next to them I feel juvenile. Despite Harlen's childish jokes.

"You do need to lie on the altar, that part wasn't a joke," says Mordecai.

I love his voice. The timbre of it. The rhythm and lilt of his slight accent. It's deeper than you would expect from looking at him, and there is a gentle rasp to it. It's very manly. Very sexy. And it seems to dance along my skin leaving goosebumps in its wake.

Damn him. Why does he have to be such an asshole? He shouldn't be this incredibly hot and an utter bastard.

He should pick one. But then again, if he was nice I'd probably just melt into a puddle of goo whenever I was in the same room. Crushes are awful and inconvenient and embarrassing. And he is like my commanding officer or something, so crushing on him would be inappropriate as well as everything else.

As my mind rambles helplessly, my body awkwardly climbs onto the altar and lies down. The stone is surprisingly warm, but it is harder than hell. I really hope I don't have to lie here for long.

Suddenly, Ri's head looms out of the darkness to snuffle at my chest. My body flinches in surprise at his sudden appearance, but no part of me is scared by this giant being. Even though his wicked looking teeth are inches from my soft, defenceless body and he could chomp me in half in one swift bite, I've never felt safer.

"Hi Ri!" I exclaim as I reach out and stroke his elegant nose.

Cool fingers run through my hair before coming to rest at my temples. Mordecai is holding my head. I shiver at the touch. It feels far too nice. But this is a magic ritual, not any type of intimacy. It's not the right time to be all touch starved and needy.

Harlen wraps his hands around my ankles. I swallow. I wish I had asked more questions about this binding ritual instead of just assuming that it was no big deal and mostly ceremonial. Surely they would have warned me about anything intense or dramatic?

Mordecai and Harlen start chanting in some language I have never heard before, which is a little bit disconcerting because I thought I knew all the arcane tongues. Their magic coils and twists around me. Seeping into my every pore, pouring into my lungs with my breaths. Ri's exotic, unhuman magic joins theirs. I feel as if I am glowing. Every cell of my body is soaked in magic. Any minute now I'm going to start floating.

Power tingles and itches along my skin. It flows from Mordecai and Harlen. It's their magic, the very essence of them. My mind interprets Harlen's as ruby red, but laced with darkness. The ruthless edge of a man that gets what he wants.

Mordecai's is pure gold. Full of flavours of love, loyalty and devotion. It's beautiful.

Ri's is so inhuman, so unlike anything I have ever experienced before that I can't interpret it at all. But I feel its strength. It's as strong as the men's.

I wonder what they can feel of me. What secrets of mine are laid bare. Do they like what they see?

"Hello Kirby," says a voice in my head. Rich and melodic and as clear as a bell.

I jump but Mordecai and Harlen hold me in place with firm, strong hands.

"Ri?" I say back silently, with complete astonishment.

"Yes."

"We can talk? Telepathically?"

"Yes."

"Oh wow! This is amazing!"

A strange rumbling sound echoes around my mind. The amusement of a dragon. It's Ri's laughter.

I glare at Harlen since Mordecai is behind me and I can't see him.

"Why didn't you tell me I'd be able to talk to Ri!" I demand, and I don't care if I'm ruining the ritual.

Harlen flushes and looks guilty. "I thought you knew."

"How the hell would I know? Not from a rider family, remember?"

Mordecai's hands disappear from my head, and Harlen releases my ankles. I guess the ritual is over. I scramble up into a sitting position. Part of me is furious at the pair of them for being such idiots for neglecting to tell me something so crucial. But I'm also full of glee and excitement. I can talk to Ri. It's incredible. It's mind blowing. It's better than all my wildest dreams.

"I can't believe you picked me!" I exclaim in delight.

Ri's amusement washes over me. *"Of course I picked you."*

A shiver of anticipation washes over me, flipping my stomach over as it passes. Is Ri about to tell me that I was the most worthy one there? The most powerful mage?

Or that he felt a soul deep connection and knew we were meant to be dragon and rider?

"You thought of me as magnificent."

I stare at the dragon. Did I just hear that right? Was I chosen merely because I flattered his ego?

"Everyone tells me I have the biggest ego they have ever known," says Ri with immense pride.

A laugh bubbles out of me despite the horror of the situation.

"You are definitely related to a cat!" I tell him.

He preens and doesn't seem the least bit offended. I guess he approves of cats. That's good to know.

"You are going to have to teach me how to keep some thoughts to myself," I say.

I hadn't *said* the ego thing, and I've only heard Ri when he has been *speaking*. I can feel a whisper of his emotions, the gentle tug of his presence. I'm aware of his vast intelligence and the experience a long lifespan has given him, but his thoughts remain his own.

"You are right, I am very intelligent and wise, but Cai and Harlen will be better at teaching you than I. They know the limitations of a human mind."

He gently butts my hand, and I resume stroking his nose.

"Okay. That does make sense," I say.

"Time to go," says Mordecai abruptly.

I look at him in alarm and with a little jolt of surprise. He is standing by my feet now, with Harlen. I didn't notice him moving from his position by my head, so either he moves as quietly as a predator or I was thoroughly distracted by talking to Ri.

"We just got here? I want to hang out with Ri." Gross, I sound so whiny.

"You're bonded now, you can talk from anywhere in the world," explains Harlen.

"But I can't give nose rubs," I protest.

Mordecai rolls his eyes and gives me the most disparaging look I have ever seen. But then Ri moves his head and butts Mordecai in the chest, hard enough to make the rider stagger back a few steps.

"Fine," snaps Mordecai. "The sacred chamber is not supposed to be used for hanging out, but whatever. Just remember to leave before the torch burns down. I don't want to have to rescue you from crawling around lost and crying in the dark."

With that, he grabs the nearest torch, turns sharply on his heels and storms off. Harlen gives me an apologetic look and a shrug before scurrying after the other rider and the only other source of light.

And now I'm alone in a vast underground chamber, with a dragon. A dragon I am bonded to. My dragon.

Definitely the best day of my life.

Chapter Six

Drifting awake in a comfy bed feels strange. I'm not sure I've ever had such a good night's sleep. And in a strange bed too. And I've never woken up so languorously. My dreams slowly drifting away, and consciousness coalescing gently and seamlessly, leaving me feeling focused and refreshed.

My new room looks great in the morning light. Grey stone walls. Narrow window. Simple fireplace. Enough room for a double bed and a chest of drawers but not much else. It's plain and basic, but it's clearly a room in a castle. I'm disappointed that the bed is an ordinary divan and not a fourposter, but maybe I can remedy that.

Shit, I haven't asked about pay. Do Dragonriders get paid? Or do we just get to live in this castle with all board and lodging taken care of? What about clothes and other necessities?

I sigh. I still have so many questions. And I need to drive back to my flat, pack up my meagre belongings and tie up my old sad life. Will I be able to do that soon? I only have enough stuff with me for an overnight stay, because that was all this was supposed to be. Not a whole new life. Not that I'm complaining. A whole new life is a hell of a lot better than a weekend job. And, hello? Dragons! And yes, very sexy men to drool over and have very inappropriate thoughts about. But mainly dragons, I am far more interested in dragons.

Gently I reach out with my thoughts. I can feel Ri's presence but I think he is sleeping. Apparently Dragons are mostly nocturnal and they sleep far more than humans. Or so Ri told me yesterday.

A sudden knock on my door makes me jump. "Come in," I say, before I remember that I'm sitting in bed, wearing my very unflattering pyjamas.

Harlen walks in carrying a tray. "I thought I'd bring you breakfast, since the scoff hall is a rowdy pit of delinquency. No need to face that hell hole until you have settled in more."

His smile is bright, but I'm not daft. I can see the lie.

"They hate me don't they?" I say flatly.

Harlen winces and carries the tray over to the chest of drawers. The food smells delicious.

"They don't hate you, they are just a bit disgruntled. When you grow up in a rider family all you dream about is being chosen by a dragon. And we haven't had any outsiders for a while."

"How long is a while?" I ask.

Harlen gives me a strange look that I can't quite decipher. "Forty-five years."

Forty-five years? I feel my eyes nearly pop out of my head. They haven't had an outsider join their little clique for nearly half a century? Oh, my god. It's going to be impossible to win them over. They are never going to accept me.

"They will love you once they get to know you," says Harlen. "You're adorable."

I quirk an eyebrow at the Dragonrider. "That's what you say about Mordecai." My hands fly to cover my mouth in sudden horror. "Oh my god, am I as bad as him?"

Harlen laughs. The corners of his eyes crinkle with amusement. "You're nothing like Cai, don't worry."

Inwardly I wince. I know what Harlen means, but damn does it speak to my insecurities. Mordecai is rude, arrogant and aloof but he is also clearly a person of importance who holds an important rank here. He is imposing and commanding. Sexy as sin and hotter than hell. I really am nothing like him and it hurts.

"Can I join you for breakfast?" asks Harlen, clearly oblivious to my inner angst.

I give him a quick nod since I can't exactly send him away after he has been kind enough to bring me food. Besides, I like his company and I have a ton of questions.

He grins, passes me a plate and then climbs onto the bed and sits next to me. There is nowhere else to sit, so it makes sense. And having an incredibly hot guy in my bed certainly feels like a win. Just a shame it's only for food.

I need to look at the breakfast he has brought me, so I don't undress him with my eyes. It looks delicious. The food. The food looks delicious, because I'm definitely not thinking about anything else.

Eggs. Bacon. Toast. Mushrooms and baked beans, as well as a sausage. A proper Full English Breakfast. Or is it a Full Welsh, since we are in Wales?

My stomach takes control of my hands and I tuck in. Harlen brings the tray over and puts it precariously on the bed, by our knees, so we can reach the orange juice and tea. This is a lovely way to start the day. Ten out of ten, would recommend. Even with Harlen being immensely distracting.

This close, I can smell him and he smells wonderful. Like sea salt and morning mist and other overly poetic and cliched things. And I swear I can feel his body heat radiating off of him and seeping into me, warming my muscles. And he is right there, inches away. His presence is all-consuming. I'm hyper aware of his every movement, his every breath. The way his bicep moves as he brings his fork to his mouth.

Oh god, I'm a sex crazed animal with a one track mind. And how much of this would Ri be hearing if he was awake?

"Can you teach me how to shield my thoughts from Ri? I don't want him to hear my every thought."

Harlen flashes me a quick smile. "Sure."

"Ri is a he, isn't he?" I ask because, thinking about it I'm not sure how I came to that assumption.

"Yeah, he is. My dragon Zh is she, but dragons are biologically both."

I give him a quizzical look as I bite into my toast.

"They mate on the full moon and they fly and fight and the winner gets to fuck and not be fucked." Harlen ends with a grin that is totally filthy.

I look away before he sees my blush. "Every full moon?" I stammer, mostly just for something to talk about.

"Yeah, every moon. But eggs are rare, and young from the eggs are super rare. The Dragons mostly just fly around and have an orgy. Best team building exercise ever."

Harlen's grin is infectious and I can't help smirking back. His eyes sparkle with naughty thoughts and I feel like a mouse hypnotised by a snake. Surely he is not thinking naughty thoughts about me? Maybe he is? Maybe he is not fussy and just likes the idea of someone new, another notch on his bedpost. My stomach flips over and I'm not sure how I feel about that. Morally, I have no objection to casual sex, I've just never done it and I'm not sure I could. But if it meant I got to have Harlen, it might be worth it.

"Finish breakfast and I'll give you some mind shielding lessons and then tonight Cai is going to give you your first flying lesson."

I can feel myself pout but there is not a damn thing I can do to stop it.

"Can't you teach me to fly?"

Harlen chuckles gleefully. "I'd love to, Kirby, but it's best to learn from the best and infuriatingly, Cai is the best rider that has ever lived."

Harlen's tone is light but I can hear his jealousy and the begrudging nature of his respect. That's interesting. Seems like there really is rivalry and some sort of manly pissing contest between Harlen and Mordecai.

I should stay well away from both of them so that I don't get caught in the crossfire. But as I look into Harlen's eyes, something tells me that it might be too late for that.

I'm already something for them to fight over.

Chapter Seven

Apparently dragons love dark underground places. It seems all those stories about caves and hoards are true, though I've yet to see any glittering piles of gold. Maybe I should ask? Though I really don't want to sound like an idiot. It's abundantly clear that I am an outsider here, I really don't need to do or say anything to make that even more apparent.

Mordecai is striding in front of me, with a flashlight this time. Dragonriders do know about electricity, which is a relief. The flaming torches must just be for rituals.

Anyway, he is ahead of me, so I can risk a sneaky look around, to see if I can spy any gold. All I see is shadows. Mordecai called this cavern 'The Stable'. It is far less imposing than the chamber where I was bound to Ri, but it's not exactly homely.

My new black leather outfit squeaks slightly and the sound is magnified in the huge space. It's so unfair. My clothes are nearly identical to Mordecai's, I was right about his leather look being functional, but he looks gorgeous in it, while I'm fairly certain I look ridiculous. Dragon riding leathers are very unforgiving. The slightly soft belly I've developed recently is easy to hide in jeans, but these damn leathers hide nothing. I'm going to have to stop eating cake and start working out.

Mordecai stops walking and his flashlight illuminates a wall of neatly placed saddles. They look pretty much like saddles for horses, more in the Western style than English, because they have prominent horns and a wide seat and skirt.

Mordecai gestures at one on a low rack, the new leather gleams, making it stand out amongst the worn leather of all the other saddles.

"That one is yours," he says imperiously.

I drift over to it and run my fingers along the exquisite craftsmanship. It's beautiful. I know it wasn't made for me, per se, but for Ri's new rider, who everyone assumed was going to be from a rider family, but I'm still moved that such a wonderful and very expensive thing was crafted for my use.

"Come on!" snaps Mordecai as he hoists up his own saddle.

I hoick mine up into my arms. It's damn heavy, and the girth is super long and trailing, which makes sense since it needs to go around a dragon and not a horse. I pull it up and pile it on top of the seat. Then I trail after Mordecai as he strides away.

After a few paces, he looks back over his shoulder. "It's easier to carry if..." he trails off as presumably he sees that I am holding the saddle just fine.

"You have a horse?" he asks instead.

I shake my head. "The foster home I grew up in had a deal with a local stable. We got to ride in exchange for helping out."

Mordecai turns his head away from me and says nothing. Not a word. I'm both incensed and grateful that he is not going down the whole, 'Oh my god, you grew up in a foster home? You poor thing,' route.

I glare at his back as we walk in the dark. He is such an annoying bastard.

The spicy smell of dragon hits me a few seconds before I see Ri. I could sense that he was close but it's wonderful to have visual confirmation.

"Good to see you, Ri," I say.

"Greetings," says Ri formally but I can sense a great deal of warmth and affection from him.

Then my attention is snatched by the being beside him. Another dragon. The only other dragon apart from Ri that I have ever seen. This one is slightly bigger than Ri and its scales are glittering emerald green but far more vibrant than that jewel.

"This is Je, Cai is his rider."

Je bobs his regal head in greeting and I feel a smile stretch across my face.

"Can you tell Je that I'm very pleased to meet him?" I ask Ri.

Je bobs his head again and then I'm flooded with Ri's pride.

"What did he say?"

Ri puffs his chest out, *"That I chose my rider well."*

I laugh and the sound echoes around the cavernous stable. Mordecai flashes me an irritated glance, but he says nothing. Instead, he moves up to Je and runs his hand along the dragon's flank. The gesture is far more gentle and caring than I expected from Mordecai, and I snatch my gaze away. It feels like I'm prying on an intimate moment.

Both dragons shift position, so that their bellies are resting on the floor.

"The saddle goes here," says Mordecai as he demonstrates by placing his saddle onto Je's back.

I assess the placement for a moment before turning to Ri and putting my saddle on him. It fits so well that I know it was made to measure.

"Here?" I check.

"Perfect," purrs Ri and it's my turn to preen. I swear I can feel his praise as a tingling sensation throughout my entire body.

He scoots back up so I can run the girth under his belly. The buckle is exactly like a horse's saddle so I have no trouble doing it up.

"Tight enough?" I ask.

"A little tighter," he says.

I laugh. So different from horses, who tend to puff their bellies out in an effort to stop the strap from fitting snugly.

I tighten up the girth and check again with my fingers to make sure it is flush with his flank but not too tight. Mordecai comes and stands behind me, so I look over my shoulder at him to make sure he is happy with what I have done.

He steps forward and checks the buckle and the tightness of the strap. He nods his approval and I feel a warm flutter in my belly.

"Do you need a hand mounting?" he asks.

"Nah, I've got this."

I really bloody hope I do, or this will be the most embarrassing moment of my entire life and that is saying something. It's been years since I've ridden a horse and obviously I've never ridden a dragon, but surely swinging up into a saddle is like riding a bike, as in you never forget? Guess I'm about to find out.

I take a deep breath, place a foot in the stirrup, grab the saddle horn and swing up. As I land neatly in the seat, I can't help but grin. I did it well and now I am sitting on a real, living, breathing dragon. Seven point nine billion people on this planet and how many of them will ever get to experience this? I am beyond privileged.

Mordecai is looking up at me with his arms crossed over his chest. There is a look in his eyes that I can't interpret.

Part of me wants it to be desire, but that part of me is ridiculous and foolishly hopeful.

"Riding a dragon is different from riding a horse. There are no reins and you don't guide with your knees either. You mostly hold on and decide on movements with Ri, just visualise what you need him to do."

I nod my understanding as I frantically try to clear my mind from horny thoughts and concentrate on what he is telling me.

"The hardest thing to adjust to is getting out of the mindset of a land animal with no aerial predators. Hundreds of thousands of years of evolution has primed you to be aware of, and think in, a flat three hundred and sixty degrees. In the air, in a battle, your world is a sphere. You need to think of up and down, as well as around."

That makes a lot of sense, and sounds very daunting. Will I ever be able to think like that?

"Tonight we are just going to go for a gentle flight. All you have to do is to try not to fall off."

I swallow dryly as my hands reflexively tighten around the saddle horn. I don't think I'm frightened of heights. But I've never been hurtling through the air on the back of a dragon before.

Mordecai walks over to Je. He swings up into the saddle with a grace that steals my breath away. Man, something about that was truly swoon worthy. Of course, all that tight leather helps.

Ri's laughter echoes through my head. Shit. I forgot to shield my thoughts the way Harlen taught me.

"Sorry!" I exclaim.

"All riders think Cai is desirable. It's good to have a healthy appetite," chuckles Ri.

The surge of jealousy that rushes through me is as unexpected as it is intense. All riders? That's a hell of a lot of competition. But I can't blame them for having eyes. The guy is like sex incarnate. It wouldn't surprise me at all if he was part incubus. So of course I'm not the only one drooling over him.

Would it make any difference if I was the only one? I'm not sure it would. I have a growing suspicion that Mordecai wants me, but I also suspect it's only because Harlen does. I'm just another toy in their rivalry. Whoever gets me, gets gloating rights. And wins the latest round of their fight. It's a very conflicting thought. On one hand, two gorgeous guys fighting over me sounds like my every fantasy come to life. On the other hand, being something for them to use and discard is grim. But I'd get some sex with a hot guy out of it, which is a win for me. Gah! I'm so confused.

"Let's go," says Mordecai.

I nearly yelp in fright as Ri starts to walk. Not a good start, he is only walking for fuck's sake! How am I going to cope with flying?

The dragons walk along for a few paces, then Mordecai waves his hand and what was a wall of stone, shimmers and disappears, revealing the Welsh night air and countryside. It looks like we are near the top of the mountain, so everything is spread out before us in a spectacular vista.

Je walks forward and just keeps going until he drops off of the edge. I see a flash of green and the pale sweep of Mordecai's hair and then they disappear out of sight. I suck in a gasp of air but before I can exhale, they reappear. Je's magnificent wings are outstretched and he is gliding through the night.

"Ready?" asks Ri.

My hands take a death grip on the saddle horn. *"As I'll ever be."*

"Lean back for the drop," says Ri.

And then we are falling. I'd scream if I could get any air into my lungs but all the air is far too busy rushing past me to pay me any heed.

I feel the moment Ri's dark wings unfold, catching the air beneath them and halting our plummet. Then we are soaring. Catching up to Je and it is glorious. Cold, brisk night air is swirling around me and suddenly the leather outfit makes complete sense. I'd be a frozen block of ice without it.

I grip tightly onto the saddle as we soar through the sky. The wind whips through my hair and I can feel the rush of excitement pumping through my veins. My first time flying on the back of a dragon and I can hardly contain my joy.

The light from the gibbous moon casts an ethereal glow over the landscape below us. The hills and valleys do look like a patchwork quilt from this height, as cheesy as that sounds, and I can see the twinkling lights of small villages in the distance.

I can feel heat emanating from Ri's body and hear the sound of his powerful wings flapping. It's an exhilarating experience, unlike anything I've ever felt before.

As we fly, I lean forward and pat Ri's neck, feeling his muscles ripple beneath my fingertips. The dragon lets out a deep, rumbling growl in response, and I can feel the vibrations through my whole body.

I can't help but let out a whoop of excitement. Despite the fact that I am a mage, this is the closest I've ever felt to being a part of something truly magical, something far bigger than myself, and I never want it to end.

Up ahead of us. Mordecai looks back. It's too far to be sure, but I think he is grinning at me and my obvious exuberance, and that feeds into my euphoria.

We continue to soar through the night sky, and I'm filled with a sense of wonder and awe. I'm not sure where we're headed, but I don't care. All that matters is that I'm flying on the back of a dragon, and it's the most thrilling experience of my life.

The tang of salt and seaweed reaches my nose. The air around me turns damp. We are near the sea. Sure enough, I see it up ahead. Glimmering a pale silver in the soft moonlight. A few heartbeats later we are over it. Ri descends, chasing Je in an exhilarating spiral until we are just skimming over the waves. I can only trust that they know how to not crash into any ships.

Soon we are out of sight of land. There is nothing but the sea below us, nothing but stars and the gibbous moon above us. Two dragons, two riders, alone in our own dominion. My heart is bursting, my mind is dizzy. This is what it means to feel alive. My entire body is vibrating with glee. I will remember this moment until my dying day. I hope there will be many many more moments like this, but this is my first time flying with Ri. It will always be special.

Ri catches up to Je, until the dragons are gliding side by side, wing tip to wing tip. I look over at Mordecai and suddenly I can't breathe. His pale hair is ethereal in the moonlight, the shadows cast by the plains of his face make him look like some sort of mythical creature. His posture as he gracefully rides Je, accents the long lean lines of his body.

I thought he was hot before, now he is on a whole new level. A demigod. A demigod of sex, lust and desire.

My addled mind finally registers his expression. He is smiling. Not smirking or sneering. A true genuine smile that shows all of his joy. He loves riding. Out here he is free. Free and happy.

It melts my heart and steals my soul. I'm done for and I don't even care. Mordecai is a demigod and I'm going to worship him forever.

Chapter Eight

The sun feels wonderful. It's seeping through me and reaching my very bones. I'm going to have to move soon because even the Welsh summer sun can burn my ridiculously pale skin, but right now I'm going to savour this heat.

The smell of the warm grass underneath and beside me is soothing. It stirs echoes of other summer days I have enjoyed. Vague memories of childhood swirl. My eyes are closed and I feel soporific.

At the other end of the quad I am lounging in, Dragonriders are also sprawled on the grass, chatting in small groups. I've avoided everyone so far but at some point I'm going to have to be brave and talk to them.

A shadow falls over me, making me shiver in the sudden drop in temperature. Seems like that moment is here. The moment I have to talk to people who hate me.

Warily I open my eyes and find two young riders looming over me. One is a girl with short spiky blond hair, the other is a boy with a buzz cut. They both look late teens and they both look like they don't like me at all.

It feels like being back in school. Or facing wild animals. Don't make any sudden movements and absolutely don't show any fear.

"Are you looking forward to the full moon?" asks the girl with a sneer that is clearly an homage to Mordecai. It's good to know that he inspires the youngsters.

"Maybe my dragon will best Ri!" gloats the boy and they both snigger maliciously.

I sit up slowly and carefully. As if I don't have a care in the world. I'm biding time while I puzzle out their words. Harlen said the dragons fly, fight and fuck on the full moon. Am I supposed to care? If this kid's dragon and Ri have fun, am I supposed to mind? Why? I really don't understand.

I shrug. "Maybe they will. No need to be childish about it."

I smile softly as they both bristle. Ah yes, teenagers hate being called childish. They are so very desperate to be seen as adults. I wish I could warn them that being an adult sucks and there really is no need to rush towards being one. But it's not as if they would listen to me.

"So you don't mind who you spread your legs for?" drawls the girl.

Excuse me? I'm so startled by her outrageous rudeness that I am rendered completely incapable of speaking.

"Ri is strong enough to beat most of the flight, but he always chooses to lose, because he loves to take it. Is that why he chose you? Because you are as much of a slut as he is?"

What the actual hell? What in the actual fucking hell is going on? What are these horrid little shits talking about? I need them to go away and it needs to happen now.

I put on my best condescending look. "I don't have time to deal with children right now. Shoo!" I close my eyes and lie back down.

They mutter something before shuffling off and the relief I feel is immense. Thank fuck for that. My heart is still pounding and I feel dizzy. I have a horrible feeling about this.

"Ri! I don't care if you are asleep! I need you to answer me!"

I sense Ri stirring sleepily and yawning. *"What is wrong?"*

I send a mental replay of what the teenagers said to me. *"What are they talking about, Ri?"*

He yawns again. *"We are bonded, my lust and desire will flood you on the full moon and you will be driven to enact what I do."*

Cold horror fills me. It runs in my veins and flows in my lungs. It settles low in my stomach and makes me want to heave.

"Are you saying, whatever dragon you sleep with, I have to sleep with their rider?"

"Yes."

I jump to my feet. *"Why did no one tell me this!"*

"Kirby, it is nothing to be alarmed about. I like to submit, you do too. It's one of the reasons I chose you."

"You could tell that about me?" My hands are covering my mouth now as if I can somehow contain this nightmare. Ri knew such intimate things about me, before we were bonded?

"Of course." The smug pride that is rolling off Ri is intense.

"Kirby, do not panic. I prefer Zh and Je and usually choose them to mate with." He sounds immensely proud of himself, as if he is presenting me with a glorious gift.

Harlen and Mordecai's dragons? A strange heat rolls through my body. Part of me is very pleased with Ri's gift. Harlen and Mordecai. Sex with them wouldn't be horrible at all. But that 'usually' in Ri's statement is doing a lot of heavy lifting. And I still don't like this. Any of this. I don't want anyone to sleep with me because they have to. And I'm rubbish and hopeless at sex and this whole thing is an awkward nightmare. I feel as if I'm going to have a full-blown panic attack.

"You do this every full moon? Lose on purpose so you get to submit?" Not that winning would make this any better.

The idea of topping whoever Ri chooses is just as horrifying.

"Yes." A wave of Ri's happiness and satisfaction washes over me. He really does love it. I can feel it. He loves the chase, the surrender, the excitement and the pleasure.

"So what you are saying Ri, is that you are a huge slutty bottom and I'm along for the ride?"

Ri's laughter rolls on and on. His amusement, mirth and glee flows through me. He really, truly cannot comprehend why I have a problem with this. To him sex doesn't come with any angst, baggage or shame. It's just fun. With no strings attached. I know his attitude is far healthier than mine but it's not like I can just switch off all my hangups.

"I hate you right now," I grumble.

"No, you don't. You love me because I am magnificent."

A huge weary sigh escapes me. He is right. I don't hate him. I can't hate him. We only met recently, but the bond allows me to feel him. To know and understand him on a far deeper level than I have ever understood and connected with any other being before. An instant best friend. One that is going to drag me into their sexcapades.

"Go back to sleep, Ri. I'm going to go yell at Harlen about this."

I feel his sleepy assent and then I turn on my heels and storm out of the quad. Where the fuck is Harlen?

Chapter Nine

I find Harlen in what looks like a tack room. The smell of leather permeates the air making the room feel warm, homely and safe. Harlen is leaning over a wooden workbench, his hand gliding over a saddle as he oils the leather. His movements are sure, confident and gentle, and for a moment I'm thoroughly distracted.

Sunlight is streaming through the window behind him, illuminating him in soft golden light and giving him a halo. His attention is fixed on what he is doing and something about that level of focus, combined with the serene look on his face, is making my insides turn all fluttery.

"Why didn't you tell me about the sex stuff!" I yell.

He is not bloody well going to distract me with his gently rippling muscles and his damn hands. No matter how seductively they are moving. I will not picture him running those frigging hands over my body the way he is fondling that leather!

Harlen looks up at me, his brown eyes wide with surprise. "What sex stuff?"

Dimly I'm aware of people scurrying out of the tack room. Good. I want to be alone with him. So I can yell at him. Definitely not any other reason. Absolutely not any other reason.

"Oh, you know!" I bite. "The whole full moon orgy thing!"

"I did tell you about that?" he says as his brows scrunch in confusion.

"You said the dragons did that, you failed to mention that riders are dragged along for the ride!"

His eyes grow huge and his face pales. His lips move a few times before he finally speaks. He does look truly mortified, and it mollifies me a little. Unless he is a fabulous actor, he did not omit this glaringly important detail on purpose.

"Oh, shit Kirby! I'm so sorry! It didn't cross my mind that you wouldn't know."

"How the hell would I know?"

"I know, I know, I'm an idiot but I'm a rider, that stuff is like saying the grass is green and the sky is up."

I cross my arms over my chest and glare at him. His excuse is pathetic, and he needs to give me more than that. He needs to do something to fix this.

"Let's go see Cai," he says as he jumps to his feet.

I blink in surprise as my mind processes his words. "Wait, what! Why?"

"He needs to know."

Harlen grabs my wrist and tows me through the castle in a blur of speed. I have a brief moment to recognise the door to Mordecai's office, before Harlen knocks on it sharply and walks in, dragging me behind him.

"Cai, I fucked up."

"What else is new?" asks Mordecai drolly as he looks up from his laptop.

Seeing him with such a modern piece of equipment, on his fancy desk, in his fancy office, in his fancy castle where he bosses a bunch of people around who ride dragons, is surprising. Surely he should work from dusty old ledgers with a quill or something?

"I forgot to tell Kirby that the bond will drive him to enact Ri's urges."

Mordecai raises one perfect eyebrow. "You are a fucking idiot, Harlen."

"I know," agrees Harlen, sounding forlorn.

Mordecai sighs and then pinches the bridge of his nose. "The bond cannot be undone."

"Hell no! I don't want it to be!" I exclaim as a frisson of terror runs through me. I can't lose Ri, I can't lose this. Nothing would be worse than that.

Mordecai stares at me with his intense gaze and I can't help flushing. "What do you want us to do?" His eyes are the colour of a stormy sea and that can't be a good sign.

I shrug uncomfortably. "I don't know."

"Kirby is gay, so that helps!" says Harlen hopefully.

I glare at him. In what possible way does that help? My sexuality has nothing to do with my consent.

"Most riders are men," he adds.

That surprises me, though thinking about who I have seen around the castle, it is blindingly obvious. I can't believe I didn't notice it.

"Why?" I ask. I'm distracted now.

Mordecai waves a hand dismissively as if the matter is beside the point, which I guess it is. "We only started presenting women to dragons recently. Yes, rider families are very sexist. Yes, we are trying to change that, but it takes time."

Okay. There is not a lot I can say to that. Especially since he is giving the distinct impression that he does not want to discuss sexism in the rider community right now.

"Do you have a preference over topping or bottoming?" he asks calmly, as if he is asking if I prefer tea or coffee.

My flush deepens until I feel like my cheeks are going to burst into actual flames.

"Bottoming," I mumble as I stare resolutely at the floor. I have no idea what he thinks the relevance is, but Mordecai asked me a direct question and I'm not brave enough to do anything other than obey him.

Mordecai sighs. "Well, at least your preferences align with Ri's, it makes this slightly less of a disaster."

"He can ask Ri not to fly?" suggests Harlen.

"That might work for a month or two, but this is Ri we are talking about."

Great. My dragon really is a slut. Strangely, I feel kind of proud of that. I like that he is so free and unapologetic about who he is. And I really like that Mordecai and Harlen seem to accept him and his nature.

But the implication that I'm like Ri is damn uncomfortable. As is Ri's earlier suggestion that it was one of the reasons he chose me. Logically, I can see the sense of what Mordecai is saying. If I was straight, I guess I'd be supernova freaking out right now instead of majorly freaking out. If I was a top, I'd be hugely freaking out. But this whole thing is still really freaky and my preferences don't change that.

"What about asking Ri to choose Zh or Je? And only one? At least for Kirby's first few moons?"

That strange heat is back, coiling low in my belly, making me feel all squirmy and out of sorts. I curl my toes and keep my gaze fixed on the floor. There is no way I can look at anyone right now, they'd be able to read me like a book.

"That might be the best we can do," agrees Mordecai with a sigh. "Assuming you would be more comfortable with one of us, since you have spent little time with any other riders yet?"

I'm squirming in earnest now. My body seems to think it can twist away from all the uncomfortable emotions swirling through it.

"I guess," I say with a shrug.

There is no way in hell that I'm confessing that sex with either of them would be a wet dream come true. It would be an honour and a privilege, if only I wasn't so nervous about sex in general and very intimidated by them specifically. Do they have mirrors? Do they understand that they shouldn't be deigning to share their bodies with mere mortals like me? Or do they understand that perfectly, but are helpless to their dragon's desires?

Oh god. This is a nightmare. A very horny nightmare. In what, four days? I'm definitely going to be having sex with either Harlen or Mordecai. I swallow tightly, that fact is going to take some getting used to.

I'm going to spiral through excitement, anticipation, dread and terror. I wonder which emotion will be winning on the night?

Chapter Ten

The full moon is here. Tonight. Not tomorrow or in a few days. Tonight. Right now. The time of waiting has passed. Four days of flight training with Mordecai, and portal closing practice with Harlen, have passed in a blur. I've had days when I've dreaded this moment and nights when I have shamefully longed for it. Now it is here I am feeling every emotion known to man, as well as several new ones that have been invented just for me.

Pacing my tiny room is not helping in the slightest, but I can't get my feet to stop. Seems I have already lost control of my body and it is barely past dinnertime.

Ri has agreed to fight only with Zh and Je and only to lose to one of them. He put on a great air of being magnanimous and benevolent about it, but he agreed. And I can sense that he is compassionate enough to not do anything that will really freak me out. He is not quite as self-obsessed as he makes out. Not that I would push that by asking him not to fly. He has his limits.

So this is the compromise. Either Harlen or Mordecai will be coming to my room, to my bed tonight. In a mere hour or two, I'll be in the arms of one of them.

A shiver wracks my body. Is it fear or anticipation? I don't have a clue. I think it is possibly both.

I've always loved the idea of sex, the theory of it anyway, but in practice it has always been disappointing. My ex was my first and my last, and he had a ton of experience. He let me know how awful I am at it. He was in the long process of teaching me before we broke up. So I really hope whoever joins me tonight is patient. But maybe all the dragon lust will compensate for my lack of skill?

Oh god, I'm going to be sick. This is going to be mortifying and humiliating.

"Nobody is bad at sex, that is a ridiculous idea."

"Ah! Ri! Get out of my head!"

"I am not in your head. You are shouting."

Oh, my god. Ri is right, I am mentally shouting. I've reached a new level of panicking.

"Sorry! Sorry! I'll put my shields back up!"

I take a deep breath and concentrate. Building my mental shields is actually calming and soothing. By the time I am done, my panic is not quite so intense.

"Sorry," I say to Ri, now that I am feeling calmer.

I sense him ruffling his wings, deep in a cavern under the castle. *"I forgive you. Emotions run high on a full moon."*

"Thank you," I say wryly.

"You will have the most wonderful time tonight Kirby, you will be thanking me in the morning."

A soft smile creeps across my face. *"I hope you are right."*

"I'm always right," Ri states confidently.

That makes a helpless laugh bubble out of me. Am I hysterical now? Gods, I hope not.

"I'm going to dampen down the bond now, I don't want your delicate sensibilities scandalised by feeling every small detail of what I am doing."

"Thanks Ri, that sounds really helpful. Have a good night."

"You too," he says, and his mischievousness is so clear it makes me laugh again.

I feel the bond fade and I don't like it one bit. Who'd have thought, I'd ever feel lonely in my own mind? But I do. It's startling how used I have become to Ri's presence. Despite his ego and his vanity, he is wise and intelligent and he has a calming, reassuring effect on me. Something like a protective older brother I guess. Not that I know what it is like to have any family.

Now that I can barely feel him, it's unsettling.

I walk over to the window. Maybe I'll be able to see him take flight. But all I can see is the deep Welsh countryside at night. In other words, just an inky black darkness. Since I'm a city boy, the sight is unnerving so I swiftly walk away. I don't need to see him, I'm just being a baby. He is still there, just not as strong as before. But still present enough that his desire is going to affect me. I can already feel arousal tickling my skin, awakening all my nerve endings.

I guess I should lube up. My stomach does a flip and my cock twitches. My body is just as confused as my mind. At least the two parts of me are agreeing on something.

I open the top draw of my chest of drawers. The sight of the giant bottle of lube Harlen gave me causes me to relive the sheer and utter mortification I felt when he presented it to me. It is a kind and thoughtful gift, I suppose. And it saves me from having to find a pharmacy, but still. Talk about awkward.

At least we don't need condoms. There are some perks to being a mage, and magic burning away diseases is not usually one I appreciate. But here I am. About to embark on a naughty night. Me. Kirby Taylor. A new shiver runs through me.

Okay, time to get comfy on the bed. My hair is still damp from my shower and it's going to get hella tangled, but that really is the least of my worries.

Lying in bed does actually feel kind of good. I wriggle around and fuss with the pillows until I am as comfortable as possible. Then I lift up the baggy tee shirt that is the only thing I am wearing. This isn't so bad. My cock is already stirring. I can't tell if Ri is flying yet and getting excited, or if it's merely that my cock knows I'm about to play with it.

I guess it doesn't matter.

The lube makes a disgusting squelching noise as I squeeze the bottle to ooze some onto my hand. But my cock knows that sound and it gets even more excited.

Closing my eyes, I lie back and take my cock in my lubed hand. Damn that feels good. How long has it been? I shouldn't neglect myself so much. I'm a young man, it's perfectly healthy to have needs.

I stroke my cock and bite my lip to stifle my groan. What should I think about? There are a couple of celebrities that usually do the trick. Or my little fantasy about being abducted by aliens who are addicted to my cum and make me spill over and over again so they can drink it.

I try to pull that scenario up but my imagination is not cooperating. It wanders. It starts to picture Harlen and Mordecai. I moan and my hand picks up the pace.

An image plays of Mordecai sneering at me. Then Harlen says I'm a good boy. Oh god. Why is that so hot? My cock is rock hard now.

I top up on lube and abandon my cock. As I sink one finger into myself, I cry out. My body trembles. It feels wonderful. I work quickly, desperate for more. The second finger feels like bliss.

My left hand finds my cock, and I groan. Why don't I do this more often? This is wonderful. A whisper brushes along my mind. Ri is flying. Ri is having fun. Lust, arousal, desire and anticipation hits me like a tsunami, washing everything else away. My hips are bucking, whimpers are spilling out of my throat, my fingers and hand are struggling to find a rhythm but everything feels so amazing. Every inch of me feels hypersensitive. Primed for sensation and pleasure.

An echo drifts down my back. A mirage of a caress. A warm body is sliding along Ri's. They are twining and dancing in the sky.

My soul twists in jealousy. I want that touch. That tenderness. That connection. I want hands other than my own caressing my body. A horrid needy sound escapes me as I add a third finger.

A soft noise makes my eyes fly open and I freeze. Mordecai is standing at the foot of my bed. He is dressed in a grey silk robe. His eyes are bright ice blue and they seem to drink in the sight of me.

"Don't stop," he rasps.

I swallow and my hands resume their work. Pleasure sparks instantly and my eyes roll back but I know Mordecai is still staring at me. Missing nothing. Observing every tiny detail.

Far, far above us, our dragons' play intensifies. A wave of Ri's need and anticipation washes over me.

I need more. I need the warmth of another body pressed against mine. I need the glide of skin on skin. I yearn to be truly filled. Stretched. I want to hear the moans of someone taking their pleasure in me.

"Please!" I whimper.

"No," says Mordecai sternly. "This might work. You might not need more."

"I do! I do! I really do! Please!"

I open my eyes to plead at Mordecai. His blue eyes flash green. His dragon is swirling through him. Je is pressed close to Ri now. I can feel it. Mordecai must be feeling it too.

My fingers and hands are frantic now. I'm so close. It feels like every stroke, every thrust is going to be the one that tips me into release. But it's not. Each one just feeds the fire burning within me. A raging storm of ecstasy that needs to be freed, but it's trapped within me burning and intense and almost painful.

"Please!" I wail. "If this worked, Dragonriders would do it all the time!"

For a moment I think the growl is one of the dragons', but it's Mordecai. His firm body, cooling against my fire, presses on top of me. His lips crash against my own. I yelp in surprise. He is kissing me?

His kiss is urgent. Hungry. Demanding. Yet somehow gentle. He coaxes me to surrender to him and I do. His tongue claims my mouth and I feel every muscle in my body melt in supplication.

I feel the kiss in my toes. It's incredible. I never knew a kiss could be like this.

His hand is on my wrist, gently pulling my fingers out of myself. I whimper and lift my hips up. I don't like the empty feeling. The brush of Mordecai's cock against my entrance feels divine. I throw my head back. He slides into me, slowly, confidently. Possessively taking me until I am his. My legs rise and wrap around his waist, I don't want him to go anywhere.

His lips move to my exposed neck, and I keen. His hips move and I am nothing but euphoria and ecstasy. Our bodies dance. Our pleasure rises. He thrusts into me and slides out. Each glide makes my body sing with sensation.

Amongst the stars, Ri is joined with Je and they are falling. Wings folded. Spinning through the night together. Their joy bursts through me and I scream as an orgasm erupts within me. Far more than a physical sensation. This scatters my mind. Ignites my soul. Disintegrates my consciousness into a thousand puzzle pieces. Sets me adrift on a dark sea of desire where nothing else exists.

A millennium later. Or maybe days. Or perhaps hours, reality starts to take shape. I'm on my stomach. Mordecai is above me and inside me. Rocking rhythmically. My cock is throbbing. The sheets are soaked. I think I've cum many, many times but a lazy lust is still burning through me.

My fingers are entwined with Mordecai's against the bed. I stare at the sight.

"You need one more, Kirby. Then you can sleep."

I whine. I can feel he is right. I can feel another orgasm growing. But I'm exhausted and overwhelmed.

Fingers twist in my hair, pulling sharp enough to make me gasp.

"Cum for me, Kirby," growls Mordecai.

And I do.

Then I let the blessed darkness take me.

Chapter Eleven

I come awake with a start. Morning light is streaming through my window, and Mordecai is standing by the foot of my bed. I scramble to a sitting position, dragging the duvet with me. Which is ridiculous because last night he saw everything.

I glance down at my baggy tee shirt in confusion. I swear it came off at some point in the night. I have hazy memories of Mordecai pulling it over my head before devouring one of my nipples and making me scream. So, did he dress me when I was out of it? That feels strangely unsettling, though I'm sure being undressed would be creepier.

I look at Mordecai warily. He is wearing a tee shirt and jeans. His pale hair is tied back. He doesn't look less stunning in casual clothes, he looks more. Because the ordinary clothes make it perfectly clear that he is not ordinary. In any way. It's almost a shame he is a Dragonrider and can't be a model. He'd rock it.

His blue eyes aren't ice bright like they were last night. They are more twilight with a hint of brewing storm. I could fall into their depths forever.

He takes my breath away. I can't believe I had sex with him. A lot of sex. A lot of mind blowing, earth shattering sex. Oh god I need to think about something else. Anything else.

Annoyingly, I can sense that Ri is sleeping deeply. Not that he'd be a useful distraction anyway, I suddenly realise. He'd be delighted that I'm thinking about sex and gleeful that I had a wonderful night just like he smugly told me I would.

"Drink!" orders Mordecai, tilting his head towards the tall glass of water that is on my bedside table and unwittingly offering me the diversion that I so desperately need.

I take it with shaking hands and gulp down half of it.

"All of it."

Mutely I obey. Once the glass is drained, I place it on the side and see a brioche on a pretty plate.

"Eat."

Okay fine. There is no need for him to be such a bossy bastard. I'm hungry anyway. Though it is really sweet of him to bring me breakfast. Yesterday, I would have sworn he'd be the type to disappear in the night, long before morning.

As I stuff the pastry in my mouth, I try to cast discreet glances his way, to see if I can gauge what he is thinking.

But his expression is just stoic. Closed, cold and guarded as ever. I've only ever seen him truly smile when he is flying.

This breakfast thing probably isn't tenderness or affection. It's probably Mordecai being dutiful. Taking care of one of his riders. He is fanatical about the people in his care. My stomach twists in disappointment.

"How are you feeling?" he says, in his delightfully rumbly voice.

"Physically or emotionally?" I ask.

He arches one perfect brow. "Both."

"A little sore," I shrug. Sore covers the emotional and physical side.

He nods as if he understands me. "Not traumatised?"

I shake my head a little too vigorously. My emotions feel raw, exposed. I feel conflicted and strange. But definitely not traumatised. Mordecai was passionate but not cruel. I probably should start thinking of him as Cai now, it seems to be what most people call him. And we had sex. If that doesn't entitle you to using someone's familiar name, I don't know what does.

Cai stares at me intently. As if the force of his glare can strip away my flesh and yield all my secrets to him. It probably can. I hold his gaze as well as I can. I want him to see that I'm okay.

Eventually he releases me. A flash of something that looks an awful lot like relief crosses his face. My heart flutters in response. He cares. He was worried. He is not as cold as he makes out.

"Alright," he snaps curtly. "You have the day off. I'll leave you to it."

With that, he turns on his heels and strides out of my room. It really does feel like he takes the sun with him. The room feels far colder without his burning presence. I shiver and then sigh.

I need to shower. I need to take my cum soaked bedding down to the laundry room without anyone seeing. Most of all, I need to process what the hell happened last night. Sex with Mordecai, I mean Cai, was incredible. Nothing at all like any sex I've had before. Is it Cai? Is it Ri's influence? Was my ex the one that was terrible at sex and I was stupid enough to believe him? There is so much to think about. So much to unpack and to get to the bottom of.

My door flings open and Harlen bounces in. He plonks himself on the bottom of my bed and stares at me with wide worried eyes.

"How are you?"

Sitting here in just a tee shirt and another man's cum, thank you very much. How are you? Luckily my brain to mouth filter works for once and I manage not to say that.

I squeak out a, "Fine," instead.

Harlen gives me a deeply suspicious look. Oh god, he is going to ask me a million questions and press me for details. I can't imagine anything worse.

"Please don't interrogate me!" I beg.

His brown eyes narrow. I stare back at him with my best pleading look. Is he jealous? Is he annoyed that Cai won this round of their rivalry? As much as I'm searching his face, I can see only concern.

I should ask him how his night went. It would be the perfect deflection, but I strongly suspect he'd gleefully tell me, in intricate detail, and there is no way I can cope with that. So I stay silent instead.

"Okay," he says with a sigh. "Shall we go get breakfast?"

I shake my head. "Cai already brought me something."

Harlen tilts his head and gives me a dazzling grin. "Told you he was adorable."

His good humour is impossible to resist and I smile back at him, even though I'm feeling slightly put out that he is not jealous. I thought he wanted me? Have I just been misreading things? Is he just friendly and nice? No, he is definitely a flirt, but I could well imagine that he flirts with everyone. I'm not special.

That thought hurts far more than it should. Who knew I was so greedy for attention? It's a disappointing character flaw.

"I need a shower," I say abruptly.

"Okay," says Harlen. "Then do you want to hang out?"

"Sure," I say with a smile, without even thinking about it.

Because I don't need to think about it. The answer is easy. I like spending time with Harlen. Even if it's only as a friend. And who knows, next full moon, Zh might win.

Chapter Twelve

A vegetable garden isn't the coolest place to hang out, but I don't care. I was a geeky, awkward child, and that never changed as I grew older. Harlen is with me, and it is a beautiful day, that's all that matters. Though, I am going to have to remember to duck back inside in an hour or two to reapply sunscreen. Being a pale-skinned redhead is such a pain in the ass sometimes. Well, most of the time actually.

I squish my baseball cap even lower onto my head, as if that will make any difference. It's hard not to be envious of Harlen strolling carefree and hatless beside me. He doesn't have to worry about sunburn, the lucky bastard.

Two women are working on one of the raised beds in the far corner of the walled garden and Harlen drags me over towards them.

As we approach, Harlen greets them with a friendly wave.

"Hey there, Rowan and Natasha," he calls out. "Mind if Kirby and I join you?"

The two women smile and beckon us over. Rowan has long blue hair that sways in the gentle breeze, while Natasha's brown curly hair bounces with her every move. They both look friendly and welcoming, which is a huge relief.

"Of course, the more the merrier," Rowan says as we approach. "We could use some extra hands to help us weed this patch."

"And it will be nice to finally meet you, Kirby," adds Natasha. "Cai and Harlen have certainly been keeping you to themselves."

I feel an entirely unnecessary blush heat my cheeks as I plonk myself down onto the ground by the raised bed. I don't know what to say to that, mostly because it is true. I've been here a week and I've barely met anyone. Harlen and Cai have definitely been keeping me away from the others and it is starting to worry me. At first I thought they were protecting me from disgruntled mages who had hoped Ri would pick them. But now I'm wondering if it is something else. Are they ashamed of me?

Rowan distracts me from my worrying thoughts by handing me a pair of gloves and a small shovel, and showing me how to identify the weeds and pull them out by the roots. It's strangely satisfying. And I'm glad to have something to focus on.

As I get stuck into the work, conversation starts to flow. A drifting lazy thing of small talk and idle chatter. I'm so glad nobody is talking about last night. Or asking me any pressing questions.

Rowan and Natasha are lovely. They don't seem to have a problem with me at all. I get the idea that they are curious about me, but they are polite enough not to pry. Maybe fitting in here won't be so difficult after all.

It seems from the chatter that neither woman is bonded to a dragon, but they were born and raised in rider families and happy with their role in the community here.

The discussion moves to pancake recipes and Natasha makes me laugh with her tales of her terrible pancake flipping disasters. A warm glowing feeling fills my chest. I'm happy. I'm content. Sitting here in the warm summer sunshine, with easy company and a fulfilling task is wonderful. It makes me realise how lonely and aimless my old life had been.

Harlen is beside me, working steadily and joining in the conversation while not dominating it. His presence is calm, reassuring. Comfortable. I feel as if I could climb into his lap and be held, and all would be right with the world. It's a very tempting thought. Even though I can still feel the echo of Cai's touch all over my body.

Another flush spreads across my face. I duck my head down and pray that everyone will just think it's the heat that is making me turn a lovely shade of tomato.

"Hey, Kirby? Shall we go inside? Looks like you've caught the sun a bit there," says Harlen.

Fuck. My. Life.

I manage to mumble something incoherent and climb to my feet. Harlen says goodbye to Natasha and Rowan, while all I can do is flash them a quick, grateful smile. They were nice to me and I really appreciate it.

Harlen takes me to the cool quiet kitchen and makes me drink a glass of water. What's with these men in my life making sure I'm hydrated? Is it a Dragonrider thing?

"Are you okay?" Harlen asks with what looks like genuine concern in his warm brown eyes.

"I'm fine."

Our gazes lock. We are all alone in the kitchen. He licks his lips as I watch, strangely transfixed by the sight. Then he takes in a breath to say something, but he merely huffs instead. Then he tries again.

"Are you looking forward to Solstice?" he says.

I blink. It clearly wasn't what he was going to say. I'll never know what that was, and the curiosity is going to eat at me, I just know it is.

"Um...I guess," I answer with a shrug.

Solstice seems to be a big deal here. Preparations were one of the things Rowan and Natasha were chatting idly about.

Harlen grins. "You are going to love it."

"I've been hearing that a lot lately," I grumble.

My mouth drops open in horror. I can't believe I just said that. That is what Ri was telling me about the full moon. Why on earth did I just say that out loud?

Harlen's eyes sparkle mischievously. I have a horrible feeling he knows exactly what I am talking about.

"You are a Dragonrider now, you are going to have to leave your prudishness far behind."

"I'm not prudish!" I snap indignantly.

Harlen laughs, "Probably not for a non rider. But you are here now, and you know, full moons happen every month."

He steps up close to me, and I swallow reflexively. As much as it confuses me when someone appears to be flirting with me, I can't shrug this off. The inflection of his voice, the gleam in his eyes, his body language, all leave absolutely no doubt. He wants it to be the full moon. He wants Ri to fight with Zh and he wants Zh to win.

I stare up at him. Okay. I'm getting the distinct impression that he doesn't even want to wait for the moon. He'd be happy to take me upstairs right now. A huge part of me is not entirely against the idea, but I don't think I'm brave enough. I need a full moon and dragons to blame my behaviour on. At least for now.

Maybe one day I'll be more confident.

"I...er...have some stuff to do," I babble. "I'll see you at dinner?"

"Yeah, sure," says Harlen.

He looks a little disappointed, but not surprised. Maybe he likes the chase and the more I turn him down, the more he will like me? Urgh. No. I hate games like that. I'm not going to play them. I can't trick anyone into liking me. They either do or they don't. Not that I have the faintest clue if Harlen likes me or just wants me. Not that it makes much difference. If I'm destined just to be the latest notch on Harlen's bedpost, then so be it. I'm not even sure if I care anymore.

I flash him a smile before I flee to my room and I'm almost disappointed that he doesn't follow me.

Chapter Thirteen

Harlen was right about the scoff hall being noisy chaos. I've ventured here a few times now, but it's still overwhelming. A large hall lined with several long oak tables, filled with rowdy riders and rider-kin.

There is a table just for riders, which I think is pompous, but I can't exactly waltz in here and demand hundreds of years of tradition are changed just because it affects my sensibilities.

Natasha and Rowan wave at me as I pass. I wave back and wish I could join them but I doggedly make my way to the rider table.

Cai is sitting at the head of the table, as usual. He is back in riding leathers and looks totally divine. Regal and aloof. Things that should not do it for me, but for some reason they really, truly do.

I take an empty seat towards the bottom of the table. Delicious dishes are already placed in the middle and it's a case of grabbing a plate and helping yourself. The informality surprised me, the first time I saw it, now I appreciate it. A stuffy, formal dinner every day of your life would be hell. Sometimes you just want to eat.

As I heap my plate high, I can feel Cai's gaze on me but I will not look at him. Mostly because I don't want to swoon at the dinner table. I really need to sit myself down and have a good long chat with myself. Do I really have a huge crush on two very different men? Shouldn't I choose one? Or is that unnecessary now that I'm a rider and as Harlen pointed out, full moons happen every month?

Come to think of it, how does that work with relationships? Do riders have relationships? Does everyone just understand that full moons mean monogamy is out of the window? Or do dragons respect their riders' pairings and similarly pair up?

As I look around the chaotic, noisy hall, I get the impression that this community being a polyamorous love fest is a far more likely answer. And I have absolutely no idea how I feel about that. I've never questioned monogamy and always just assumed it was the only option. Of course I knew other types of relationships existed, it is just that exploring them never crossed my mind. Until now.

Could I have both Cai and Harlen? And not have to choose? A warm tingling feeling coils in my guts. But I'm really getting ahead of myself. I'm pretty sure both men are interested in taking me to bed, but while Cai already has, thanks to the full moon, nobody has hinted at a relationship. At all. It's probably not the way things work here.

Okay, that thought makes me sad. Seems I might be on board with polyamory, but not friends with benefits. I think I want a deeper connection. I want love.

I snort over my mouthful of mashed potatoes. Now I really am being ridiculous.

I swear I feel Harlen's presence a few heartbeats before he jumps into the seat next to me. His sudden appearance scatters all my thoughts. He smells good. He is close enough that I can feel his body heat and I love it. It's a part of him that I get to keep.

He flashes me a quick grin that makes my heart do a somersault. I'm probably staring at him with a stupidly soppy expression. A movement at the head of the table catches my attention and before I know what I'm doing, my eyes are locked with Cai's. The look he gives me is truly terrifying and my heart starts racing for an entirely different reason.

I blink, and Cai's face is blank, stony. Emotionless. Did I just imagine that? What the hell is going on?

Before I can ponder that question, a wail fills the air. Startling me and stealing my full, undivided attention. It's screeching, insistent. A sound of impending doom. I freeze in fright but everyone else jumps to their feet and swiftly, efficiently, files out of the hall.

Numbly, I trail after Harlen.

"It's an attack," he confirms.

Suddenly Cai is right beside us. "You haven't finished your training, Kirby. You are staying here."

My feet take root to the floor beneath me. My mouth drops open. I want to say something, anything. But what is there to say? Cai is right. If I went, I'd be far more a hindrance than a help. But staying here while they go off into actual real-life frigging battle is awful.

As I stand here, riders walk past me. I'm like a stone in a stream. My gaze is fixed on Harlen and Cai's backs until they are out of sight. They don't look back. They don't offer any words of comfort. Nor should they. They have far more important things to deal with than my emotions and I'm not so needy as all that.

The hall feels empty with all the riders gone. The atmosphere is sombre and quiet. Rowan and Natasha are by my side and I didn't even notice them approaching.

"What do we do?" I ask in a hoarse rasp.

Rowan sighs. "There is nothing we can do."

"Except double check the infirmary is stocked and ready," adds Natasha.

"And wait," says Rowan.

I think I'm going to be sick. I feel too hot and too cold. My head is spinning. Cai and Harlen are in mortal danger. What if they get hurt? What if they die? Is there really nothing I can do?

"Be calm, Kirby. We have done this thousands of times," says Ri.

A strange whimper escapes from my throat. *"You are going too?"*

"Of course. I always fight. All dragons do, bonded and unbonded. Soon you will be able to join me and it will be glorious."

"Be safe," I plead, pouring all my love, hope and concern into my words.

Ri rumbles his appreciation and I feel him take flight. I hastily withdraw from the bond as much as possible, the last thing I want to do is distract him and cause a disaster.

This is awful. Three people that I care about are in mortal danger and all I can do is stand here. Useless, helpless. I have an urge to run up onto the battlements, part of me seems to think that watching will somehow help. As if my sight has any super powers. But I wouldn't be able to see anything anyway. Dragons fly far and fast. The fight is not going to be over the castle.

The only thing I can do is wait. Wait and make preparations for their return.

It may be nearly summer solstice and the shortest night of the year, but tonight is going to be the longest night.

Chapter Fourteen

I'm standing outside the stable, hopping from foot to foot. Ri has already told me that the battle is over and everyone is fine, but I need to see the humans with my own eyes.

A sea of riders stream past me. It's just like Cai and Harlen to be last, I can just imagine them lingering back, making sure everyone else is okay. I know that part of it is their job, but more of it is just who they are as people. It's both endearing and infuriating.

Finally they emerge, strolling side by side. They've both shoved their riding goggles onto the top of their head and pulled their masks down under their chin. They are looking a little tired but none the worse for wear after being in a life and death situation. It's so good to see them. I'm so relieved and thankful. The thought of anything happening to either of them is unbearable.

I fling myself at Cai and wrap my arms tightly around his slender body. He tenses and I can feel his shock and surprise, but I don't care, I'm not letting go. I need to feel him. I need undeniable proof that he is alive and unharmed.

Slowly Cai's arms move to wrap around me. His body relaxes into my embrace. I give him an extra squeeze before bounding away to throw myself into Harlen's arms. Harlen chuckles and hugs me back warmly.

"We are fine, Kirby. There was no need to worry."

I pull back a little, just enough to scowl at him. "You try waiting and then tell me how you like it!"

"Alright, fair enough," he agrees, with just enough solemness in his brown eyes to appease me.

I step back, grab his hand and then Cai's and start pulling them both towards their bedrooms, which are thankfully next to each other.

"I've got food and water in your rooms. And I've run you both a bath," I tell them.

We reach Harlen's room first and I shove him unceremoniously into it before continuing to drag Cai to his room, since Cai is the one who is going to be stubborn about being taken care of.

I push Cai onto a sitting position on the bed. Then I drop to my knees in front of him. My hands find the zipper on the inside of his long boot. The damn thing is stiff. It glides down reluctantly, the soft noise echoing around the quiet of the room. As it finishes its journey, I look up at Cai.

He is staring down at me, his head is tilted forward just enough so that his long blond hair tumbles over his beautiful face. His eyes are Mediterranean blue in this light and his look is intense. Regal. Haughty. He looks every inch like some fey prince and it feels right that I am kneeling before him.

My breath hitches. My heart flutters. I've pulled off one of his boots and now I'm just kneeling here holding it, like it is some sort of trophy.

This wasn't meant to be a sexy thing. I meant it to be a caring and nurturing thing. I thought they would be tired after the battle, and looking after them was a small way I could help. But now the atmosphere in Cai's room is charged. It feels like the slightest movement will cause enough friction to ignite the very air.

"You look good on your knees," he whispers.

His words dance along my skin, leaving goosebumps behind. His tone is mocking. He is being demeaning, insulting even. But I don't care. I think cruelty is his love language. I don't think he knows any other way to be.

Slowly, purposefully. I put the boot down and then place my hands on his still booted calf. I hold his gaze as I languidly slide the zipper down. The metal parts seductively. Responding to my glacial pace. If he wants to play games, I can play.

I watch as his eyes darken and a faint sheen of colour brushes his pale cheeks. Satisfaction coils within me. A dark and hungry thing. I've won, and it wants more.

Cai reaches out. His fingers trail along my cheek before drifting down to cup my chin. Helplessly I lean into his touch. His eyes darken even more. He smells of dragon, sea spray and cool night air. I'm not sure who is winning now.

Harlen's voice sounds out behind me, all drawling and suggestive. "Cai and I could share a bath, save water."

Cai's eyes blaze with fury. "Fuck off!"

I look over my shoulder to see Harlen's reaction. The Dragonrider is leaning in the doorway, arms crossed over his broad chest. His dark eyes are sparkling and a smirk is on his lips. He appears completely unphased by Cai's wrath.

"Spoil sport," he says lazily.

Cai glowers at him. I can't tell if he is angry at the interruption, or the lewd proposition. It's possibly both.

"I made sandwiches!" I interject brightly. "I wasn't sure exactly when you'd get back, so I didn't want anything to get cold but I thought you'd be hungry because the siren sounded at dinner. There are some in your room too, Harlen."

I gesture at the plate of sandwiches on Cai's bedside cabinet. Neither of them even glance over, but the tension has definitely dissipated. Despite them both being locked in some sort of silent staring contest.

"Harlen, I've already run your bath. Go get in it before it gets cold."

Harlen lets out a large dramatic sigh. "Fine," he says before turning and walking away with the silent grace of a predator.

I knew it. I knew he was a player and that his attention was not just for me alone. Seeing it still stings though.

"Is he always such a giant flirt?" I ask without thinking about it.

I wince. Whatever the hell I just witnessed, it wasn't harmless flirting and Cai being annoyed by it. I may be jealous and feeling slighted to be robbed of his attention. But something far deeper was going on between Harlen and Cai. Something that I cannot begin to decipher.

I cast Cai a worried glance, and then stare in disbelief at the soft tender smile that teases the corner of his lips. "He likes to take his chances. He thinks if he shoots enough shots, some are bound to hit."

Now I'm super confused. Cai was acting as if he was about to murder Harlen a heartbeat ago and now he is acting as if he is fond of the other rider. What the hell is going on?

I'm burning to ask if they have ever slept together, either because of the full moon or just because. Ri said he preferred Zh and Je, but I don't know if that has ever included at the same time, or if Zh and Je have been together. Ri would be happy to tell me in glorious detail, I'm sure. But that feels too sneaky and prying. A little sordid. I don't need to know. It's none of my business.

"Can I get you anything else?" I ask as I climb to my feet.

Cai shakes his head. "Thank you for all of this, Kirby."

I flush. It's only sandwiches and a bath and seductively removing boots. Cai's tone is implying that I have bestowed a great honour upon him, when really, it was all the least I could do. Well, the whole boot thing was a bit over the top, but nevermind. It can't be helped now.

"You're welcome," I mutter as I flee.

If I stay any longer, I might end up doing something that I would regret in the morning. Or not regret at all. And I don't know which would be worse.

So fleeing is definitely the best option of them all. Flee and play it safe. That could be my motto. Except I don't think I like it anymore. I think it might be time to embrace a new philosophy and live a little.

If only that thought wasn't so scary.

The dream swirls through me, vivid and vibrant. Full of colour and sound and exquisite detail. I feel as if I am there. Invisible, unseen. A voyeur of the utmost skill.

It looks like Cai's bathroom. Candles are dotted around the bath. Bubbles fill it. Harlen is leaning against the back, Cai is in front of him, leaning back against Harlen's wet naked chest.

Cai's skin is glimmering pale against Harlen's olive tones. Harlen's hands are under the bubbles, unseen, but I'm sure I know what they are doing. Cai's expression is telling me that. His head is tilted back, resting on Harlen's shoulder and facing the Dragonrider. His eyes are closed. His jaw is slack with pleasure.

Harlen is staring down at him. His eyes darker than the abyss. A smile tugs at his lips. Pride, possessiveness and a ruthless predatory satisfaction.

Cai is soft and pliant in Harlen's arms. Every muscle is lax. He has surrendered completely and Harlen is loving it. Devouring it as if he is a dark demon and Cai's submission is his sustenance.

My body shudders. It groans and writhes, and I am pulled back to it and consciousness. I gasp in a breath of air. It's quiet in my room and the dawn light is streaming through my windows. It was very late when the riders returned from battle, I can only have been asleep for an hour.

My pyjama trousers are wet. What the hell? A wet dream? I haven't had one of those since the early days of puberty. But the aftershocks of arousal and release are still trembling through me. And I can still vividly recall the dream. I swallow. That was a very hot dream. No wonder I came in my pants.

Unless it wasn't a dream? Could it have been a psychic projection? Goosebumps erupt all over my skin. The scene I just witnessed could be playing out in reality right now. The urge to jump out of bed and run to Cai's bathroom is strong, but I resist. If it is really happening, I was not invited.

A shaky breath escapes me. I hate that thought. I never thought I was the jealous type before but now I'm seething with it. Jealousy, rejection and yearning all have their toxic claws in me.

Okay, I need to take a deep breath and get my shit together. It was probably just a dream. No need to be hurt over a flipping dream.

I wriggle out of my soiled pyjamas and chuck them on the floor to deal with in the morning. Well, more morning than dawn, because I am sure as hell not getting up right now. I'm going back to sleep in my cold, lonely bed and dealing with reality later. Much later, hopefully.

I close my eyes, but it is a long time before I find sleep.

Chapter Fifteen

"You're late," Cai's snide tone nearly makes me jump out of my skin.

I whirl to find him lurking in my doorway, dressed in his riding leathers and sneering at me condescendingly.

"Sorry," I mutter. "I can't get these goggles to fit."

I turn back to the mirror and continue fiddling. I've flown a few times now, but this is the first time Cai has decreed that I need goggles. Apparently we are going to be going fast enough to need them. I'm both excited and terrified.

Cai strides up and stands in front of me, super close. So close that if I stuck out my tongue, I could lick him. Would that make him mine? According to the TickTock videos about, 'If I lick it, it's mine', it would. I stifle my inane giggle, as he ruthlessly pulls my goggle straps around.

An image flashes of my bathtub dream and I flush. There is no sign of that man standing before me. This man would never be all soft and pliant for anyone. It had to have been a dream and I'm in awe of my subconsciousness's imagination. Where did it get the idea of Cai surrendering from? How did it know it would be hotter than hell?

Cai steps back and stares at me with narrow eyes. I swallow. Please, please don't tell me he is a mind reader. Cold horror and terror snakes in my guts. If he heard that thought...

"There," he says.

Only now do I realise that I am looking at him through my goggles. My hands fly up and run along the leather straps. Snug, secure and comfortable.

"Thanks!" I say.

Cai nods sharply, turns on his heels and strides away. I jog to catch up with him. Somehow his order to come with him was clear in every line of his body, without him saying a word. And, as usual, I find myself helplessly obeying him. I should hate it. Part of me does despise it. But it's also super sexy. And apparently I have a filthy mind. He is the flight commander, people are supposed to obey him without thought. It's how fighting forces work. Trust me to turn it into something kinky.

Except I swear I never had a kinky thought in my life until I came here. I sigh. Well, Cai and Harlen are both ridiculously, stupendously good looking. It's not like I can help it. I'm only human, it's not my fault.

Harlen is waiting by the entrance to the stable, leaning back against the wall with his arms crossed. He looks damn fine in riding leathers too. These men are going to be the death of me, I swear. I'll swoon one too many times, or my heart will flutter too hard, and I'll drop down dead.

Harlen grins and gives me a wink, as if he knows exactly what I am thinking. He pushes himself off the wall with an effortless grace that does not help my imminent demise in the slightest.

He falls into place beside me as we walk over to the saddles.

"You alright?" he asks.

"Yeah. You?" I manage to say.

I think I pulled it off and sounded normal and not like a thousand naughty thoughts are running wild through my mind, having a little orgy of their own.

"Yeah, all good here," he says easily.

His tone gives nothing away. Oh well, if he has discerned my filthy imagination, it seems he is not going to use it against me. Thank heavens for small mercies. Perhaps he feels empathy towards a kindred spirit, because I'm quite sure that nearly all his thoughts are positively depraved.

We grab our saddles and walk down to where our dragons are waiting. As soon as I see Ri, I can't stop running over to him. He lowers his head so I can give him the head rubs I know he adores. We exchange warmth and affection through our bond but no actual words.

I breathe in spicy dragon scent and feel calm, content. Happy. After a moment my skin tingles with awareness. Someone is watching me. I look over and meet Cai's intense gaze. He is standing so close to Je that they are touching, from Cai's shoulder, to his ankle. One of Cai's hands is idly stroking Je's eye ridge, but the rider's attention is fixed on me. I can't read his expression. I have no idea what he is thinking, but his scrutiny is unsettling so I turn and face Harlen instead.

Harlen is in front of Zh, scratching her nose. His brown eyes are filled with love and it is touching to see. Zh's golden scales gleam even in the dark of the stable. She is a fair bit larger than Ri and Je, and ferocious looking. Ri told me that she has never lost a fight, and I can see why.

"Let's ride," orders Cai as he swings up into Je's saddle.

The movement is fluid, confident. Graceful. It makes me feel entirely too hot. Every frigging time. I need to remember not to watch.

Cai start's adjusting his goggles and mask and I haven't even put Ri's saddle on yet. I jump into action and complete the task quickly.

"Tighter," says Ri.

"Are you sure?" I ask. *"I don't want to hurt you."*

"And I don't want the saddle to slide mid flight and send you hurtling to your death," answers Ri while adding a very vivid and entirely unnecessary mental image of me falling through the sky.

"Are you saying you wouldn't catch me?"

"I'd try."

"You're worried because you think you would fail?"

Ri huffs. *"Of course I wouldn't fail. I never fail. Just tighten the girth!"*

I laugh and do as I'm bid. Then I swing up onto Ri's back. One day I'll make it look as good as Cai does, but for now I'm just glad I can make it without huffing and puffing.

Harlen is mounted too and putting his goggles on. I missed him vaulting onto Zh's back, which is probably a good thing. Too much swooning before flying can't be good for one's ability to not fall off. I have no idea why a good-looking man swinging up onto a dragon's back is so alluring, but I just have to accept that it is and deal with the effects.

Je and Cai drop first. Then it's my turn, and Harlen is going to bring up the rear. I don't think I'll ever get used to the stomach churning, terror-inducing drop. But it is exhilarating and well worth enduring for the joy of flying that follows.

Ri's dark wings unfurl and I can't help yelling in exuberant glee. Ri's amused pride swirls around me. Up ahead of us, Je's emerald scales are glimmering against the cloud filled dark sky. Ri banks to get us into formation. I look over my shoulder. Harlen and Zh are right behind us. We are in a staggered line, like migrating geese. Not that I would ever tell Ri that.

I can already smell the ocean. Dragons have cloaking magic, anyone looking up at the night sky won't see a thing, but over the sea is even safer. There are no eyes out here to somehow see past the magic.

The few ships that pass through the seas off the coast of Wales rarely have people on deck. Freight ships and fishing vessels navigate by machinery and the crew are too busy working to star gaze.

Pale water soon appears below us. The waves mere wrinkles at this height. The dragons catch an updraft and the steady beat of their wings still to a glide. Silence embraces us. The wind ruffles my hair and whistles over my goggles but there is no other sound. I'm gliding through the night sky with Ri and I feel a part of it.

Cai and Harlen and their dragons are with me. And I feel I am a part of them too. I'm not an outsider looking in. We are together. We are one.

This moment feels magical. I feel as if I might burst with happiness. For the first time in forever, I feel the warm glow of companionship. I feel like I belong. I have a place in this crazy world. I am complete.

"Ready?" Cai's voice cackles in my ear and I jump.

I'd forgotten about the ear piece. Mages are a practical bunch. If technology can do the job well enough, we won't waste magic on it. It's good to know that riders are just mages with wings.

"Ready," I confirm.

A portal opens up above me. Sunlight streams out of it. I see green trees at an angle that is disorientating. I urge Ri closer, by sending him a mental image of where I need to be. Two flaps of his huge wings and we are there. A quick flurry of hand gestures from me and the portal slams shut. I'm about to gloat, when I spot another portal at my three o'clock. Bastards. I should have known they wouldn't make this easy.

Ri rushes towards it. I haven't even closed it when another one appears. Breathless and dizzy, Ri and I race across the sky slamming portals shut as quickly as Cai and Harlen can open them.

I've lost count but I think it's been six, when something falls shrieking past me. It has a long inhumanly thin body covered in clammy looking grey skin. White feathered wings are folded along its back. It's diving head first towards the earth.

"What the fuck is that!" I exclaim.

"A mirage of a tylwyth," says Cai.

"Nobody said they were so fucking ugly!"

Harlen laughs.

"Catch it!" barks Cai.

"You heard him, Ri!"

Ri folds his wings and we fall. My stomach rises up into my throat and I can really see why we need goggles and masks. The force of the air rushing past me is intense. I wouldn't be able to breathe or see without protection.

Ri turns as we fall, so we are spiralling down the sky. It's dizzying and exhilarating. We gain on the tylwyth. The creature twists and turns, trying to evade us, but I have it. I cast out a blast of magic and disintegrate it.

Dark wings unfurl, ceasing our plummet, and my guts lurch again. But I don't hurl. I'm exhausted, spent and dizzy. Breathless but exuberant. I did it. I can do it. Surely they will let me join them in a real battle soon?

Zh and Je drop down beside us. The dragons spread out their wings and we fly side by side, wing tip to wing tip as the waves swell below us.

Harlen grins at me and Cai nods. They are both proud of me. I could burst with pride.

As one, we turn towards home. And that thought stretches my beaming smile even further, so much so that my face hurts. Home. The most beautiful word in any language. And one I can finally use.

I've been tossing and turning in my bed for what feels like forever. Whatever I try, counting sheep, stilling my breathing, meditating, I just can't find sleep. I'm too wired after that glorious fight and mock battle. It's going to be dawn soon, so I might as well just give up and go for a walk. The view from the battlements is stunning and I can watch the sunrise. That will be a perk of being awake at this ungodly hour.

I throw my tatty robe over my pyjamas and head out. Ri is fast asleep, deep in his lair in the mountain. It would be cruel to wake him just to keep me company. So I leave him be.

As I make my way up the stone spiral staircase, I'm startled by a dark shadow up ahead. It's Cai. He is dressed in jeans and a black hoodie and is inexplicably on his knees. He is breathing heavily and those look like tears on his face. His pale hair is all mussed.

"Cai?" I ask tentatively.

"Fuck off," he says without force but his voice is hoarse and rasping.

He flows to his feet and barges past me, fleeing down the stairs and back into the castle. Should I go after him? I get the distinct impression he will disembowel me if I do.

My feet carry me up onto the battlements while my mind puzzles what it just saw and what my best course of action is. Then my gaze falls on Harlen, leaning on the battlement wall, enjoying the view and a vape. The relief I feel is immense. He will know what to do. I hurry over to him.

"I just saw Cai on his knees, he looked like he had been crying and his voice was all hoarse," I blurt.

Harlen turns to face me. Even in the dark, the mischievous gleam in his eyes is clear.

"Sounds like someone was a very lucky bastard."

I stare at him in confusion for a heartbeat and then my stupid, ignorant mind catches up. My hands fly up to cover my gaping mouth. Oh, my god. Cai gave someone a blow job. That's why he was like that. Oh lord, given the state of his hair, and his tears, it was quite a...um vigorous one.

All sorts of very naughty images start to crowd at the corners of my mind, gleefully wanting to torment and horrify me.

"Lucky bastard? Does that mean you are jealous?" I babble in an effort to keep my vivid imagination at bay.

Harlen chuckles. "You've seen Cai, right? With your eyes? Who wouldn't want that?"

I drop his gaze. All sorts of emotions swirl through me, all of them unpleasant. Most of all I'm jealous. In all sorts of ways. I'm jealous that I wasn't the one having fun with Cai, even though I can't imagine doing that to him. I'm jealous that Harlen likes Cai. Both because I want Harlen to like me, and because I like Cai and I don't want anyone else to.

A warm gentle finger slips under my chin. Harlen gently tilts my head up so that my gaze finds his. His eyes are dark and all too knowing.

"I have room in my heart for more than one person," he says softly.

My breath hitches. Does he mean that, or is it merely a damn good line? I stare into his eyes and try to read him. He seems extremely sincere as far as I can tell.

I step back to free myself from him and try to gather my thoughts. My heart is racing and my palms are sweating. I lean on the wall next to him and look out at the view, but I don't really see it.

"It was you, wasn't it?" I state.

Nothing else makes sense. The way Cai and Harlen are with each other. The way I found Harlen here, not far from where Cai was. The fact that I cannot imagine Cai dropping to his knees for anyone else on the planet, let alone in this castle. It all makes too much sense. Harlen gets Cai to surrender to him, and Cai hates it. And loves it.

Harlen takes a big drag of his vape and blows the smoke out into the pre-dawn air where the breeze carries it away.

"Yeah, it was me," he confesses calmly while staring out at the view.

I knew it.

So where does that leave me?

Chapter Sixteen

I don't know how I let myself be talked into this, but here I am, sitting on the end of my bed while Natasha and Rowan braid my hair and weave flipping white flowers into it. Apparently everyone wears flowers in their hair for Solstice. I'm not entirely convinced that I'm not being pranked but hey, this bit is nice.

We are chatting and drinking actual mead, of all things. Natasha has some weird music playing softly on her phone. It feels like being a teenager getting ready for a night out. Not that I went out when I was younger. Or had the type of friends I could get ready with. But this is what I imagine it is like.

"Your hair is so gorgeous," sighs Rowan wistfully. "You should wear it down all the time."

I snort in disagreement and take another sip of mead. The drink is sweet and not unpleasant. It's definitely going to get me drunk. Is everyone going to get drunk? That is certainly the impression I am getting and it can't be a good idea.

"What if the tylwyth attack?" I ask.

"There has never been an attack on Solstice, it's one of the reasons it is a sacred night."

That doesn't sound good. It sounds like a perfect ploy to lull riders into a false sense of security. Wait a hundred years, and then invade. An impeccably played long game.

"We think their portals don't work on the Solstice," says Natasha. "Well that's what tutors taught me when I was young, anyway."

She sees my worried look and smiles.

"Don't worry, every region has a fortress that stays on watch. It was our turn last year. It was horrible. So this year we are partying our asses off!"

A party does sound fun. Though I'm sure drunk people, and this huge fire they are planning on having isn't the safest of combinations, but hell, these people ride dragons and fight battles with alien fairy demon things. I guess a little bonfire isn't very intimidating after that.

"You know," says Rowan and I can tell by how she is slightly slurring, that she is already a little tipsy. "Most people go topless and paint their chests with blue spirals."

My mind goes straight to Cai and Harlen. Are they going to be shirtless? Is Cai's pale, dancer's body going to be adorned with body paint? Is Harlen's bronzed six pack going to be on display? Suddenly I'm very keen for this party to get started.

"I've got wode, we could paint you," offers Natasha.

I shake my head in horror. No one needs to see my premature dad bod. Cai makes pale look good. On him it's all ethereal starlight. On me it just looks pasty and unhealthy and almost neon. Scattered with some random freckles.

Natasha shrugs at my refusal and pulls her top off. My eyes are bugging out I swear, but I can't help it. I've never been in the same room as real life naked boobs before. I snatch my gaze away but not before I see enough to confirm something. I am definitely one hundred per cent gay.

Rowan opens up the pot of blue body paint and starts decorating her friend. They continue chatting and drinking, as if nudity is no big deal. So I guess it isn't for riders and rider-kin. Gosh, If everyone is going to be half naked tonight, lord knows what I am going to do with my eyes. I'm just going to have to stare at the fire.

Stare at the flames while standing there awkwardly, and angst over Harlen and Cai and their situationship and what it means for me. Yep. That definitely sounds like me at a party. The exact opposite of the life and soul. So, I guess that makes me what? The death and void of the party?

I snort laugh to myself and take another sip of mead.

A short while later, Natasha and Rowan decide it is time to leave. As I stand up, dizziness rocks me. Shit, this mead is good stuff. I'm already drunk.

My friends lead me out of the castle and down the hill. Drums beat out and beckon me to join them. I feel the pulse beating through me. It feels like the heartbeat of the land and it calls me to match my own rhythm to it.

We pass a rocky outcrop and come to a flat piece of ground that overlooks the lake and the mountains beyond. The little plateau is dominated by the hugest bonfire I have ever seen. It has to be at least eight foot tall.

What looks like a hundred people circle it, all looking wild and free. Body paint, naked skin, feathers and masks. Those with drums are moving exuberantly. Others are dancing. Joyful whoops echo out to the night air. The sight takes my breath away.

As I step up to the flames, I see Cai. His chest is bare. Blue spirals adorn his skin, snaking over his abdomen and pecs. His pale hair is loose, tumbling down to his slender shoulders. A crown of blood-red flowers sits on top of his head. Tight black leather trousers cover his long legs. Far tighter than his riding leathers. These sit so low on his hips it's obscene. I love them.

My gaze rakes over him. Over and over again. Drinking in the sight, consuming it. I have never in my entire life seen anyone look so incredibly hot. All the things I've heard before, like not being able to breathe, blink or move, are apparently really true. I always assumed they were metaphors and used them as such, but now my muscles are turning to jelly, probably from the lack of oxygen caused by me being unable to breathe.

Cai has to be a fey prince. I can no longer believe he merely looks like one. And I really can't believe I've had him. Me. Kirby Taylor, has taken the cock of the fey prince of sex.

He is not even looking at me, he is staring into the flames instead and the reflection of the fire in his eyes is adding to his otherworldly appearance. He lifts an impressive looking silver tankard to his lips and takes a deep drink. I wonder if it's mead and if his lips will now taste like honey.

Someone crashes into me and squeezes me into a bear hug. Harlen's familiar presence engulfs me. All muscles and warmth and a manly musk.

"Kirby!" he bellows happily. "Have some cider!"

He releases me and thrusts a tankard into my hand. It sloshes everywhere and the sweet smell of fermented apples washes over me. I take a sip and gag. It's like vinegar and battery acid.

"That's disgusting!" I splutter.

Harlen laughs. "I made it myself. Been brewing it since last autumn."

"I...I mean it's very strong," I stutter, floundering desperately.

A strong whack on my back makes me stagger. "It's not meant to taste nice, it's meant to put hairs on your chest!" yells Harlen gleefully.

His brown eyes are sparkling. Tiny yellow flowers are scattered through his chestnut curls. My gaze drifts lower and discovers his naked, bronzed and muscular chest. Blue spirals circle his nipples and draw attention to them. They are beautiful nipples. All dusky and inviting. I lick my lips and tear my gaze away, back up to his face where I find him smirking at me.

"I don't want hair on my chest," I say.

Harlen's eyes light up. "Oh, so you're smooth skinned? I've been trying to imagine red chest hair."

His gaze drops down to my crotch briefly, before flicking back up to give me the filthiest wink in the history of winks. Letting me know without a shadow of doubt that he has been thinking about far more than chest hair.

"You look damn fine with your hair down," he adds with an evil, appreciative leer.

My cheeks heat. Spectacularly, by the feel of it, I look away from Harlen, only to be caught by Cai's gaze. He looks murderous for a moment, then he looks away and the dismissal hurts more than his fury. Is he mad that Harlen is flirting with me? If so, who is he jealous of? Or is he like me and feeling envy from all directions?

Surely it's far more likely that he wants to keep Harlen to himself?

I'm startled out of my morose thoughts by someone running around the fire handing out unlit wooden torches. Harlen grabs one and hands it to me with a flourish. I grin at him.

Everyone else starts lighting their torches from the bonfire, so I copy them. The heat of the flames is intense. I feel it soak into my skin.

Suddenly, everyone starts whooping and yelling and inexplicably running away from the fire. Harlen takes my hand and pulls me along as we chase after them. I'm running down a Welsh mountainside in the middle of the night whilst holding a flaming torch. Surrounded by hundreds of people, and a truly gorgeous man is holding my hand. How did this happen? How did my life come to this?

The night is lit by a myriad of flames that seem to swirl and snake down the mountain as people pick their way through the rocks. The dotted lights shine through the darkness and through it all the deep drums keep up their rhythm. It's a truly awe-inspiring sight. A wondrous phenomenon to be a part of.

Far away, over the sea, Ri pauses in his fishing to send me a warm feeling of love. He is happy that I'm happy. And I'm happy that he is happy, flying free with the other dragons, feasting and frolicking. I send him a wave of warmth and love back and then my thoughts are scattered to the wind. We've reached the lake shore.

A huge maze spiral has been carved into the earth. The crevices filled with sawdust and set alight. Creating a blazing, flaming effigy. Some people circle the maze, others start to dance through the fire, following the snaking, twisting path. Harlen pulls me towards the entrance. The drumbeats fill my ears. Wild feral cries fill the air.

"Wait!" I yell. "We need Cai."

Harlen looks back over his shoulder at me. "He won't want to come."

"Yes, he will."

My eyes find him easily. He is standing not too far away. Somehow separate from everyone else despite being surrounded by people. He is staring at us intently. I hold my hand out to him and beckon. He hesitates briefly and then, with a few swift strides, he joins us and takes my outstretched hand.

I turn back to Harlen to give him a satisfied 'I-told-you-so' grin, but his attention is fixed on Cai. Harlen's face show surprise, but his eyes are burning with intense joy. My heart flips over at the sight.

Harlen lets out a loud whoop and runs into the maze, yanking me with him. As I'm pulled forward, I jerk Cai with me. The three of us stumble and stagger into the burning maze.

We dance, twirl and twist through it. Keeping our feet moving fast enough to not get burned. Everything is cast in orange and yellow firelight and the very air shakes with the beat of the drums. Harlen is laughing, his dark eyes brimming with glee. I look back at Cai and he is smiling too, his blue eyes flashing like sapphires. Both their hands feel warm and strong, and I love that I have one of each.

Harlen is pulling me and I am pulling Cai. I'm laughing and laughing.

We reach the centre of the maze and spin around. Then we dance gleefully out. As we leave the maze, I'm breathless and giddy. Harlen is snatched away by a crowd of friends and Cai says something about water.

I'm dizzy and the flames are hot. The drums are reverberating in my ears. I need some fresh air. I stagger away to the lakeshore. Hells, I'm drunker than I thought. It's cool by the water. The gentle ripple of tiny waves against the shore is soothing. I can breathe. Big lungfuls of fresh country air fill me. I still feel the thrum of the drums. I can see the orange glow from the flames. But I can't see anyone down here. I am alone.

The heat from the fire starts to leave my body. My heart rate is slowing. I'll go back soon, but this is nice.

"Kirby?" rumbles a voice by my ear.

A yelp of fright escapes me, and I stumble. Strong hands take my shoulders and steady me and I find myself standing chest to chest with Cai.

"Are you alright?" he asks.

I stare up at him. His face is all shadows and contours in the dark. His eyes are as colourless as a storm laden sea.

I nod. His lips take my own, and he does taste like honey. His arms encircle my back and press me even closer to him. The kiss is tender, deep. Almost desperate. Cai kisses me as if he is starving and I'm the only source of sustenance in the universe. His lips are soft, yet urgent and the feel of them sliding against me awakens every nerve ending that I posses. The sensation of his kiss sparks along my entire body.

I melt into it. Surrender to it completely. My arms wrap around his neck so I can cling onto him and try to stay upright. His tongue claims my mouth and I whimper.

I'm hard, so very hard, and I can feel his erection pressing against my stomach. I fall to my knees before I've consciously decided to. But I want to. I really want to. I want to take care of him. I want to serve him. I yearn to give him this. I look up at him and find him staring down at me with a feral gleam in his eyes. He is hungry for this, hungry for me.

Battling with his tight leather trousers takes far longer than I want it, to but finally his cock is free.

I admire it for a moment. It's a thing of beauty. Full and thick and long and I can't believe I've had it inside me. No wonder I was driven to the very limits of ecstasy. This cock before me is sheer perfection.

I place my hands on his legs for balance. Mead and cider is swirling through me, making me unsteady and I really don't want to fall.

I wet my lips in preparation and take just the very tip of him into my mouth. He groans and runs his hand over my scalp. I swirl my tongue over the head of his cock and exult in the soft cry he gives me in return. Then my mind ceases to work. I suck, I lick, I devour. The weight of him on my tongue, the slide of him over my stretched lips. I'm in heaven, I have to be. No moment this perfect exists on Earth.

"This is very distracting," grumbles Ri.

"Revenge for every full moon!" I snap at him.

Ri huffs and pulls away from the bond. Leaving me in peace to worship Cai's glorious cock. I lose myself in the glory of it. My own cock is straining painfully against my jeans.

I hear footsteps behind me and I'm about to pull away in horror, when Harlen's warm presence kneels behind me. His body is chucking out fierce heat, and it's solid and comforting against my back. His hands reach around me, undo my jeans and free my aching cock to the cool night air. My whimper is muffled by the cock in my mouth. Harlen's strong, confident hand wraps around my cock and he starts to stroke it with exquisite skill. Jesus Fucking Christ. How am I not going to bite Cai? Somehow, I manage to wail with my mouth stuffed full.

Harlen's hands on me while my mouth is full of Cai is a dual delight I can barely cope with. I'm going to be utterly destroyed. This bliss is beyond anything I have ever imagined.

"You are doing great, Kirby," whispers Harlen in my ear. "Give him a little more suction."

I do as I'm bid and Cai lets out a strangled moan.

Harlen sighs. "See, he likes that. Go a little faster."

I comply and Cai whimpers.

"See how his legs are shaking? He is very close. Flick your tongue across his slit and get ready to swallow."

I obey and Cai grunts. His cock throbs in my mouth and then he spills down my throat. I want to try to drink it all but Harlen tightens his grip on my cock and my mouth falls open with a cry. I collapse back against him, my head lolling against his shoulder. He pumps and pumps. One hand grips my hip tightly, holding me still so I can't thrust into his movements, I can only take it. My body is trembling. My muscles are quivering. Obscene, carnal noises I did not know I could make are spilling out of me non stop. I know Cai is right in front of me, watching everything. Watching me become completely unravelled and undone.

My orgasm detonates with the force of a thousand burning suns. I am incinerated by it. There is nothing of me left. I have been smited by the angel of lust and I am nothing but screaming euphoria, until I slip into darkness.

I float peacefully for a while. Then I hear voices. Feel movement. I'm in Harlen's arms, being carried in a bridal carry somewhere. I can't open my eyes but I don't need to. I'm safe. I'm happy.

"Are you sure he has only passed out?" asks Cai.

"Yes, stop fretting," I can feel Harlen's voice through his chest. It's a nice feeling, as is the gentle sway of him walking.

"Fucking hell, Harlen. We just assaulted him!"

Harlen chuckles. "No, we didn't"

"He is so drunk, he has passed out! He wasn't in any state to give consent."

"Cai, calm down. He wants you, he wants me. It's all good."

Cai makes a noise of disbelief and derision. I want to speak, I want to reassure him that I'm more than fine, that it was wonderful, but I can't move. I can only listen.

Harlen lowers me down and soft sheets caress me. I murmur but I still can't do anymore than that.

"Why are you taking his trousers off!" snaps Cai.

"Because they are wet from kneeling on the ground," answers Harlen wryly.

Cai makes a strange strangled sound of mortification and Harlen chuckles again. Warm hands manoeuvre my body. It's strangely endearing. I feel cared for.

"He is so beautiful," remarks Harlen.

What the hell? Okay, I have to be dreaming. No way is this real.

"And so fucking sweet, he doesn't belong here!" says Cai.

"That's not very nice," says Harlen.

"You know what I mean!" Cai sounds exasperated. "This place is going to ruin him, look what we did to him tonight!"

"Stop moaning, Cai. You got your cock sucked, Kirby got to blow his load. I'm the only one not taken care of here."

"Fuck off!" snarls Cai and I can hear him back away as if he has suddenly realised that Harlen is a dangerous predator.

"Cai, Cai, Cai," sighs Harlen. "Why do you always put up such a fight, when you always cry out yes in the end?"

"No," says Cai sternly and the command in his voice sends shivers down my spine.

Harlen, however, seems immune to it.

"The harder you make me work for it, Cai. The harder I will fuck you," promises Harlen.

Cai draws in a soft shaky breath and then silence falls. I want to see them staring at each other but my eyelids won't budge.

When Harlen speaks, his voice is gentle, tender even. "There is nothing wrong with being vers and a switch, Cai."

"I'm not...I don't..."

It's strange to hear Cai sounding so flustered and flummoxed. The power Harlen has over him is astonishing. No wonder there is a love hate thing going on.

"Hmm mm," teases Harlen. "Let's go to your room and you can tell that to your pillow while I fuck you into the mattress."

The noise Cai makes speaks directly to my cock. It twitches and tries to stir. I try to call out as I hear footsteps leaving my room, leaving me alone. I want to see what Harlen just promised, I want to watch that. Fucking hell, I want to witness that more than I have ever wanted anything. But my treacherous body carries me off to sleep instead.

Chapter Seventeen

Rugby. I can't believe I'm playing rugby. Well, apparently it's a crazy, lawless bastardised version, but since I haven't got the faintest clue about rugby, or any sport, I'm none the wiser.

Cai is forcing me to play with other riders. Team building, tactic practice and exercise. I call it torture. It's June for Pete's sake. I'm not made for running around in the midday heat. I'm sweating and I'm the only one wearing a baseball cap, but I daren't take it off for fear of being burnt to a crisp by the sun.

Cai is standing to the side of the pitch. Hatless, probably even sunscreenless. He probably doesn't get burnt, even though he is nearly as pale as me. The sun is probably too scared to touch him. No, Cai gets to stand there all perfect looking with his hair pulled back and casual white tee shirt and jeans that would look simple on anyone else but look Met Gala level stunning on him.

He has a whistle around his neck and occasionally shouts commands but mostly he is watching us intently, while leaving us to it.

Out of the corner of my eye I see something hurtling towards me, I turn and catch the ball before I realise what I'm doing. A surprising bolt of pride and joy sparks through me, but it is short-lived as every pair of eyes on the pitch turn towards me with blood thirsty intent.

Oh shit.

I run. I duck. I dive. The world blurs around me. I hear people breathing close to me yet somehow I avoid being thrown to the ground. I slide across the white line at the end of the pitch and punch the air in glee. I'm far too breathless to shout.

The whistle blows. "Take a break for lunch," says Cai.

Not even a 'Well done, Kirby.' Or, 'Good match.' Nothing. He is such an asshole.

I stomp over with the others to a grassy bank shaded by trees. Cai stays on the opposite side of the pitch and gets his phone out and starts typing away. Work emails are my best guess. I can't imagine him having Instagram. He probably thinks it's far beneath him. Which is a shame. He'd be hugely popular.

Tegwyn hands me a bottle of water from the blue plastic cooler and I take it gratefully before flopping on the grass. I hate to admit it, but this enforced sporting activity is allowing me to get to know other riders.

Tegwyn is tall and lanky. With brown hair and eyes. His friend, Dai is shorter with a softer body shape. Carl has the darkest skin I have ever seen on a person and a truly awesome laugh. They are all in their mid to late twenties and have been friendly enough. I don't think any of them have family members that were hoping to be chosen by Ri. Unlike the other rugby players.

At least I'm hoping that's why the others have been a bit standoffish and wary of me. I don't think I've done anything to annoy anyone.

Dai hands me a ham sandwich and I tuck in eagerly. It's nice lying in the shade and not flipping running up and down. My lungs are calming down and sweat is cooling on my back.

My gaze is drawn back to Cai. He is still working on his phone. Is he going to come and join us when he is done? Am I ever going to get to talk to him about what happened on the solstice and assure him I'm absolutely fine about it? It's been three days now and an opportunity hasn't arisen. The thought of having to seek him out purposefully to have such a chat is making me feel a little queasy, but it is the adult thing to do.

"You'll wear your eyes out if you keep staring at him like that," says Tegwyn.

I stare at him in openmouthed horror for a moment before fixing my gaze on my bottle of water. Have I really been so shamelessly, blatantly obvious? That is so cringeworthy.

"It's pointless anyway, the Flight Commander doesn't mess around with his subordinates and everyone here is his subordinate," adds Tegwyn around his mouthful of sandwich.

Images of being on my knees by the lake flash through my mind. I know I didn't dream it so Tegwyn's assertion is clearly not true.

"Except for full moons, but those don't mean anything, he probably didn't even see you. He was Je and you were Ri. You'll get used to it," explains Dai with a hint of a condescending tone that gets my back up. I ignore it though. It's not worth making enemies over.

Movement at the far end of the pitch catches my eye and I look over to see Harlen jogging up to Cai. He is wearing a sleeveless loose cotton top and his biceps are on full display. His dark curly hair moves as he jogs, and it truly is a sight to behold.

Cai looks up from his phone, and the two men start talking. I'm concerned for a moment, but it soon becomes clear from their body language that whatever Harlen needs to talk to Cai about, isn't terrible news. Probably just every day Dragonrider stuff.

"What about Harlen?" I hear myself asking and I wince but it's far too late. The words have escaped me.

Dai laughs gleefully. "Harlen will fuck you, he will fuck anybody."

"But he is second-in-command? If Cai can't, then why..."

"World of difference," says Tegwyn with a shake of his head.

"But it won't mean anything either," says Dai.

"Why not?"

"Because he is madly in love with the Flight Commander. Has been for years."

That news sinks into my heart and my soul. I feel cold in the midsummer sun. I feel sick. I feel as if I might shatter into a hundred thousand pieces.

"What does Cai think of that?" I croak.

"He loves him too, you should see the way he looks at him sometimes, when he thinks no one is looking," whispers Tegwyn conspiratorially.

"So why aren't they together?" I say except it comes out more like a distraught wail.

My stomach is churning. My palms are sweaty. I always thought tales of people dying of a broken heart were utter nonsense. Now I'm not so sure.

"Because they are both top dogs, dominants, alphas, whatever you want to call it," says Dai.

I blink. That is not true either. Well, not all the time anyway. Has no one else seen Cai with Harlen? Does no one else know what I know? Have I really blundered my way into discovering such a secret? This is a lot to take in. A huge responsibility. I'm like an open book, it's impossible for me to keep secrets, but I'm going to have to. I can't betray Cai.

"Well, apart from on moons when Zh bests Je. Then the Flight Commander is super pissed at Harlen for days afterwards and in a foul mood generally. Fouler than usual," grumbles Tegwyn.

"But the point is, it would never work between them. They both need someone to boss around," says Dai.

It takes every ounce of my self control not to leap up and go all Katniss Everdeen and yell across the pitch that I volunteer as tribute. They can both boss me around in the bedroom all night, every night. I don't mind at all. I don't mind in the slightest.

Hope blooms within me. Chasing away all my earlier despair. This could actually work. I could be their missing puzzle piece. Cai can take control of me. Harlen can dominate both of us. Everyone can be happy and get what they need. It could be perfect.

Now I just need to convince Cai and Harlen of that.

Chapter Eighteen

I know damn well that a full moon happens every twenty-eight days, I'm a mage. The luna cycle has been a part of my life forever. I just never expected twenty-eight days to pass so swiftly. All the training, the eventful Solstice, getting to know some of the other riders and rider-kin, has all conspired to speed time up I swear. There was also the day Harlen insisted on driving me back to my shitty flat to collect my things, because he declared that my car was a death trap.

That memory makes me smile. I've never understood the appeal of road trips before, but Harlen made it fun. But he also contributed to the days passing by in a blur and now suddenly it is the full moon again and I'm pacing anxiously around my room.

"Ri, I'm begging you to please choose Je or Zh."

Ri gives me the psychic equivalent of a heavy sigh. *"I've agreed."*

"You said maybe!"

"Stop fussing, Kirby. Everything will be wonderful."

I groan and cover my face with my hands. Memories of the last full moon are starting to shiver down my skin until I can almost trace the echo of Cai's touch. Has it begun already? Is Ri's arousal overflowing and seeping into me, awakening my own and calling it out to play? I guess I'll never know. All I do know is that I'm horny. Horny and nervous. Not my favourite combination of emotions.

I shut Ri out as best I can. Then I flop belly first onto my bed. It's still early, there is no need to prepare myself just yet. I can just lie here and drift on the currents of lust that are building in strength within me.

I can't decide if I want Cai or Harlen more, but it doesn't matter. I know I want both of them. I want us to be a poly, three-way, or whatever it is called, something. A relationship would be my first choice. Seems I'm still foolish enough to believe in love. But I'm not so naïve to assume that will be an outcome. I'd take a situationship. I'll take anything. Maybe I'm overly soppy, but I just want the three of us to be happy. And I do think we could work well together.

Maybe Ri is right, and tonight will be wonderful. If he chooses Je or Zh, it will be an opportunity to get closer to one of them. It does feel a bit sneaky and underhand, but I've never claimed to be a saint.

In my defence, I did try to convince Ri to not fly tonight. To be one of the dragons on watch in case there was an attack, but Ri was outraged at the suggestion. Apparently, attacks on the full moon are exceedingly rare, and basically, my dragon is a horny sex addict. Not that he described it that way, but that is the gist of it.

I shiver. A wave of cold air is washing over me. The castle is old and draughty, but not that draughty. Which means only one thing, Ri has taken flight.

A strange moan pours out of my throat. I'm still apprehensive but I'm also filled with a dark and terrible excitement. My body is responding, and it is eager, so very eager.

Dreamlike erotic images flow through my mind. It feels as if I am floating on them. Lost in them. Pieces of myself carried away and scattered by the ebb and flow of the currents. Until I can't tell where I end and the dream begins. Time floats away and I have no idea how long I have been writhing on my bed for.

"Hi, little one," purrs Cai's voice behind me.

I whimper and clutch the sheets. Yes. Yes. Yes!

His confident hands knead my ass cheeks and the sensation pulls an awful sound from me. I don't remember getting naked, but I'm so very glad that I am.

Fingers trail down my crack, to my hole. My entire body shudders. My cock is leaking onto the sheets beneath me.

"Did you forget to prepare yourself for me?" whispers Cai softly.

My body squirms. I want to apologise. I want to beg for forgiveness, but I can't form the words. Let alone remember how to talk.

"It's alright, little one. This way is more fun."

My ass cheeks are spread apart and something hot, wet and soft is lapping at my entrance. Pleasure shoots like electricity from the nerve endings there, racing to every part of my body until I feel as if I am alight. I yowl and whine and twist. Cai chuckles darkly and effortlessly holds me in place.

His tongue strokes and strokes. And I yell and yell. Then he pierces me and I see stars. Having a tongue inside me feels incredible. I never knew such bliss existed on this mortal plane. It's blowing my mind to discover that the human body is capable of such pleasure.

I want this moment to last for eternity. I want to lie here while Cai ravishes me with his tongue, until the last star burns out.

His tongue disappears. I whine at the loss and lift my ass up towards him in supplication. But he ignores me.

"Roll over."

I scramble to obey. As my eyes focus on the sight of Cai, naked and kneeling on the bed beside me I gasp. His expression is hungry and intense. His eyes are wide and dark and in their depths I see flashes of emerald green from his dragon.

"Hold on to the headboard," he growls.

Wordlessly I comply. As my arms rise up above my head, his eyes flash with appreciation.

He positions himself between my spread legs and stares down at me. I swallow and shiver. In this moment, I am utterly his to command and I think he knows it.

"Hold my gaze," he says. "Keep looking into my eyes. If you look away, I'll stop and not give you what you want."

I whimper and nod my understanding. A tiny, miniscule part of my mind that is still functioning, argues that Cai is driven by his dragon as much as I am and he wouldn't be able to stop. But that voice is easy to ignore.

Cai grins at me. A truly evil, filthy grin. My cock twitches in response and my legs spread even further.

The blunt head of his cock pushes at my entrance. My eyes want to roll back, but I don't let them. I stare at Cai steadily as he works his way inside me and breaches me. I let him see all of me. I allow him to witness his actions unravelling me. I show him how overwhelming it is to be filled, taken and possessed.

He slowly slides all the way in. I dimly register that his cock is smeared in lube but I'm far too bombarded by other sensations to fully register it. All I know is that Cai is inside me and it feels wonderful.

I stare up at him in awe. He is an angel or a demon or god that I could worship forever. His lips quirk in a wicked smirk and he rolls his hips. My head tilts back and I keen to the stars, my gaze has been torn away but Cai doesn't reprimand me for it. He just thrusts into me with a magnificent rhythm that rearranges my brain cells along with my guts.

My cries of joy are my prayers to the moon. My carnal worship. Cai is a priest of lust and I am enlightened. And utterly devoted.

Suddenly everything stops, and he pauses within me. My eyes snap back to him and widen in shock. Harlen is looming over his shoulder. He has a handful of Cai's hair and is forcing his head back. Cai's eyes are half closed and the look of sheer bliss on his face, takes my breath away.

"Hey, Brat," whispers Harlen. "I hope you weren't stubborn and didn't prepare yourself. Cos that's not going to stop me."

Cai's cock throbs deep within me and he gasps.

Harlen moves and then sighs. "Ah, good boy."

Cai lets out a single strangled whimper. I watch, completely transfixed as Harlen works himself into Cai, while Cai is still impaling me. Not a single thought is running through my head. My every brain cell is utterly devoted to observing this awe-inspiring sight.

Harlen grunts, and his dark eyes flash. I think he is all the way in. Cai's hands are on either side of my head. I don't know if he is holding Harlen up, or if Harlen is keeping his weight off of both of us, but I'm not being squished. Just delightfully filled.

A cry escapes me as Cai moves and he fills me deeper. Harlen is thrusting into him and the force of it is driving Cai into me.

I can't stop moaning. The feel of Cai filling me and sliding in and out, is a physical euphoria. The knowledge that Harlen is filling him, is mentally going to destroy me. I can't ever recover from this. It is impossible.

Grunts and moans fill the air. Along with the sound of flesh upon flesh. It's carnal and erotic and I adore it. Our bodies find a rhythm, we are dancing as one. The oldest dance. The most sacred dance. It rolls on and on and my pleasure grows and grows.

Harlen thrusts deeply and groans. He has cum deep inside Cai. Cai shudders and the force of it spreads into my body.

Suddenly, there is a flurry of movement, and I am left empty and alone. Harlen has pulled Cai back into a sitting sprawl against him. His legs are spread. His head tilted back by Harlen's grip on his hair. His eyes are closed and he is panting.

"Fuck him," orders Harlen as he stares at me.

"W...what?" I stammer helplessly.

Harlen's tanned hand drifts down to Cai's pale pink nipple and caresses it. Cai arches his back and gasps. Harlen has hooked his knees under Cai's and is spreading Cai's legs wide. Wide enough to expose his hole. His hole that is wet and open from Harlen.

I lick my lips. Arousal is running through my veins instead of blood. I've never topped anyone and suddenly I can't think of anything I want more.

"Ri isn't..." I trail off uselessly.

I can't really tell what our dragons are doing exactly, but I'm sure I would feel that.

"But Zh is, and Cai needs it."

Cai's cock does look very full. It's standing proud against his abdomen and weeping pre-cum. Harlen lowers his head and bites Cai, just where his neck and shoulder meet. Cai cries out and lifts his hips up.

I crawl forward. My cock is throbbing. I want to cum so bad it hurts. I want Cai with every fibre of my being. Harlen is continuing to torment Cai's nipples and suck at his neck. Soft, helpless whimpers are spilling out of the flight commander's mouth. His head is now lolling against Harlen's shoulder. He is beautiful like this.

"Cai? Do you want this?" I whisper.

I'm not sure if he can hear me. He seems very lost in a sea of lust, arousal and desire.

He nods. The movement is jerky and uncoordinated, and he doesn't open his eyes. But I'll take it. I shuffle even closer and line my cock up. I take a deep breath and then I'm easing into him. He is hot and tight around me. He is moaning for me, canting his hips up for me. I sink even further, feeling him open up and stretch around me. His body accepting mine.

My hips take over. Instinct drives me. This primal dance is etched into my soul and my body knows exactly what to do. I surrender to it. I'm breathing in ecstasy and exhaling euphoria. Pleasure is burning through me, irrevocably transforming every part of me.

I'm fucking Cai and it truly feels like a religious experience. I've attained Nirvana. Time ceases to have meaning. Nothing and no one exists except this bed and the three of us. We are our own universe.

Cai clenches around me. His back arches as every muscle in his body goes rigid. I can feel him quivering around my cock. As he cries out his orgasm, my own overtakes me. Joy and blinding light are the only things I know.

An eternity later, I can dimly fathom that I'm collapsed on top of Cai and Harlen. I'm panting like oxygen is going out of fashion, and sweat is cooling along my back.

Harlen chuckles darkly. "That was a good start to the night."

The noise that comes out of me is part whimper, part protestation, part need and hungry anticipation.

Harlen laughs again, and I know I'm done for. But what a glorious way to go.

Chapter Nineteen

Sunlight is trying to blaze through my eyelids. I'm warm, floppy and sated. Utterly unready to wake up and face reality. So I roll over, and smoosh into someone. Someone with a long lean body. I open my eyes and stare at Cai as he opens his. Brilliant sapphire regards me for the briefest of moments and then he is rolling off of my bed and fleeing. I grab his wrist and he freezes.

"Wait!" I beg.

I know I have nanoseconds to plead my case, to give him a reason to stay. A thousand possible sentences flow through my mind. 'Are you okay?' 'Did you truly consent to that?' 'Do you hate me now?'

They are all useless. None of them will work. Then inspiration strikes. Cai hates being fussed over, but he is dedicated to caring for others.

"That...um was my first time topping."

He turns his head and looks over his shoulder at me. His eyes are wide and shocked and his face paler than usual.

Shit. I didn't mean to make him feel bad. That wasn't my point at all.

"How are you feeling," he rumbles.

"Fine!" I say hastily. "But I could do with a hug."

Cai moves and before I really know what is happening, I'm on my side and Cai is curled up behind me, his arm around my waist. I place my arm on top of his and snuggle into him. I hate lying, but hugs are always nice and I'm damn sure he needs this, so it's all good.

"Are you okay?" I ask tentatively. I only just got him to stay. I don't want him to run away.

"Yeah," he sighs, but he sounds sad.

"You don't like bottoming?" I ask, even though my stomach is churning. I'm pretty sure he does, but the idea that he is merely driven by his dragon is awful.

He takes a deep breath. "Real men don't. They only tolerate it if their dragon makes it absolutely necessary."

"Who told you that?" I splutter as my outrage grows.

"My father," he says so quietly that I only just hear him.

Fury and rage swirls through me. I scramble out of Cai's embrace and reach for my phone on the bedside cabinet. He watches me in bemusement as I fumble with it, but thankfully it doesn't take too long to find a picture of one of my acquaintances. I show my screen to Cai, who blinks at it. The man I am showing him is huge. Tall, insanely ripped. The very definition of shit brick house.

He is sitting on his Harley in his biker gear and looking like the baddest ass to ever walk the earth.

"You going to tell him to his face that he is not a real man? Because he is a bottom."

Cai laughs, and the good natured sound fills me with glee. It's working. I am making him feel better.

"Not unless I had Je with me," he confesses.

I grin at him, and then jump out of my skin as my bedroom door flies open. Harlen strolls in carrying a tray. The bastard kicked my door, he is such an animal. Though the three tall glasses of orange juice that I spy look promising, so maybe I will forgive him.

Harlen pauses for a moment. His dark eyes flicking between Cai and me as we sit on the bed. An ecstatic, grateful look crosses over his face before disappearing and being replaced with a smug smirk.

"Breakfast!" he calls gleefully as he clambers onto the bed with his tray, revealing a plate heaped high with buttered toast. I grab a piece and a glass of orange juice and settle back against the headboard happily.

Cai accepts some breakfast too and I'm relieved that he is going to stay. The three of us, sitting on my bed in my tiny room feels wonderful. I could get used to this.

We eat in silence for a moment. My bedding is going to get covered in crumbs, but I guess after last night, a few bits of food aren't going to make much difference. Next time we should use someone else's bed and their sheets can get destroyed.

Next time. I nearly choke on my toast. I can't believe that thought just crossed my mind. It is rather audacious. I shouldn't be so presumptuous. But maybe I am being entirely reasonable?

As I eat my toast, I cast discreet glances at the two men in my bed. They had a good time didn't they? They'd be up for a repeat, surely? Or are they just following their dragons' whims and have no actual interest in me?

Gah! I hate being so whiny, insecure and needy. It's pathetic. I hope some of Ri's blazing confidence rubs off on me, I could really, truly do with it.

Harlen leans forward and tucks a strand of Cai's hair back behind his ear. Cai freezes for a moment and narrows his eyes, but then he resumes chewing his toast without saying anything.

I hide my grin in my orange juice. Those two are the sweetest pair I have ever seen. I swear Harlen is utterly devoted to Cai, and that Cai adores Harlen, but he is too stubborn to admit it.

Harlen glances at me and gives me a naughty wink that promises all sorts of depravity. My stomach flutters in anticipation and my hole clenches in fear. I don't blame it. Discovering that Harlen has a monster in his pants was quite the revelation. It's broad as well as long and taking it is difficult and divine. No wonder Cai complains about it, and secretly worships it. I'm right with him there.

Last night, with Harlen stretching me to nearly breaking point while Cai exquisitely sucked my cock, I seriously thought I was going to die. And I was all for it. It would have been a perfect way to go.

At one point, I thought we had destroyed Cai. Harlen was fingering him and stroking him, while I was sucking on one nipple, while twisting the other. I remember glancing up at Harlen and seeing his expression of pure rapture, and wondering if he was about to expire too.

I think all three of us had multiple near-death experiences at various points throughout the night.

Sex is incredible. I think it might be my new religion. I can see myself becoming as obsessed with it as Ri is. But only with these two men. Only Cai and Harlen. I don't want anyone else. I'm sure some people would say that I should live a little, explore my sexual awakening, but my heart knows what it wants. It wants Cai, Harlen and me, together.

"We've got work to do," says Cai, interrupting my soppy thoughts.

Harlen groans. "What's the point in being the boss if you can't give yourself and your besties the morning off?"

Cai narrows his eyes. "You are not my bestie," he snaps as he flows off of my bed and scoops his robe up off of the floor.

It's hard not to ogle his ass as he bends over, but I catch Harlen doing the same, so I don't feel too bad.

"Kirby can have the day off," says Cai.

"Hey! That's not fair!" protests Harlen.

"He is still new to all of this, you're not."

Harlen puts on an exaggerated pout, and Cai shakes his head in annoyance before striding out of my room without a backward glance. I try not to feel sad about it. He stayed even longer than I had hoped he would. It's a damn good start.

Harlen sighs heavily and stands. "See you later, Kirby."

His smile is genuine, and his eyes are kind. I smile back at him and then he is gone. Leaving me alone with my filthy sheets.

Chapter Twenty

Rowan and Natasha are both far too good at pool. If Tegwyn and Dai weren't also getting thoroughly thrashed, I'd feel utterly humiliated.

It's noisy in the rec room, several other groups are in here, but I'm getting used to it. The idea of living by myself in a tiny flat is starting to feel bizarre. Cooking for one. Watching television alone. The unending silence. The weight of nothing but your own company. I never want to experience that again.

Natasha takes her shot. The white ball slams into the maroon ball and effortlessly rolls it into the far right pocket. It's flawless. She makes it look easy.

A siren wails, cutting through the air. Scattering my thoughts and reverberating in my skull. All other noise in the rec room ceases as everyone stops what they were doing. The crowd files out calmly. My heart is hammering, I'm feeling the exact opposite of calm. Cai hasn't officially declared that I'm ready to fight, but I'm sure I'm very close to the expected standard. He has seemed pleased with me the last few times we have ridden.

I follow everyone else to the kit room and start pulling on my riding leathers. Agitation is itching along my skin. Will the riders on watch manage to hold the fort until the rest of us get there? I don't know any of them well, but my concern still spikes for them. The idea of anyone getting hurt is awful. As for the thought of a tylwyth getting through... I can't even go there.

My leathers seem to creak loudly as I head towards the stable. Heralding their newness, and therefore my inexperience. I can't tell if my trepidation is because Cai might not let me fly, or because he might.

As I reach the stable, I see Cai standing by the entrance with his arms crossed, watching all his riders efficiently flow in. His fierce blue gaze flicks to me and I freeze mid step. Other riders swarm around me while I suffer Cai's intense attention. My palms are sweating and I want to swallow but my throat is too tight. I stare back at Cai and wait.

He nods. A brief decisive gesture that sets my feet in motion. I hurry past him. I'm both relieved and terrified. Luckily, my muscles have learnt this routine and they pick up Ri's saddle without needing a single conscious thought from me.

I find Ri amongst all the other dragons in the huge, dimly lit cavern easily. He is thrumming with excitement and anticipation. There is not a grain of concern or fear in him anywhere and it makes me feel better. He clearly has faith in my abilities, because he is brutally honest and if he was at all worried, I'd know about it. As well as being able to sense it.

I swiftly attach the saddle onto my dragon's back. Then I swing up into place, put my goggles and mask on and try to brace myself. I'm about to go into battle. On a dragon. It's surreal. A large part of me cannot comprehend that this is really happening. It feels like a dream.

I glance around and see that Harlen is astride Zh, right at the front of the stable, the closest to the drop. He doesn't look back at me, but his presence is still comforting.

Je is saddled and next to Zh. Waiting patiently for his rider. I think we all are.

A few heartbeats later, he appears. Cai strides over to Je and vaults onto the dragon's back in a fluid move that looks inhuman. My stomach flutters and my chest tightens. Every fucking time. I really, truly must remember not to watch.

Ri chuckles, and I give him the psychic equivalent of the finger. It merely amuses him even more.

Cai lifts his hand up and as one, all the dragons step forward. Je and Zh drop first and then it's a steady stream until it's Ri's turn. I close my eyes and cling on tightly. It's soon over and we are soaring through the night sky, drifting into formation.

There are six bonded dragons in front of me, with Je at point. Six more are behind me. Unbonded dragons fly beside us, scattered around our tight formation.

I want to whoop with joy. We feel like a pack, a tribe, a family. I adore it. I am part of a flight. And it means the world to me.

The dark night air is brisk, even though it is full of the scents of summer, warm grass and sweet flowers. But the clean, crisp smell of the ocean is rapidly taking over. We are flying further than I've flown for training and despite the fear and the sombreness of the occasion, I can't help feeling exhilarated.

A flash of green arcs across the sky. Beautiful and ethereal. The Northern Lights. I've always wanted to see them and now I get to do it from dragon back.

"What do you think the Northern Lights are?" asks Ri.

"Um, magnetic something or other bouncing away solar flares?"

Ri snorts in indignation. *"They are the portals, ignorant human."*

What the? I blink through my startled astonishment as my mind yet again readjusts everything it thought it knew about the world. Then I grumble, *"Not my fault no one told me."*

"I suppose so," concedes Ri.

I huff and don't answer him. I always thought the Northern Lights were pretty and spectacular. A wondrous natural phenomena. Discovering they are a dangerous threat is a bitter pill to swallow and I don't like it.

"Get ready!" warns Ri and my heart rate triples. I can feel it in my throat, hammering away.

I cast my gaze across the sky, looking for portals as I summon my magic and get ready to start closing them. Focusing makes my nerves fall away. I'm good at magic wielding, I love it. Doing it from dragon back, in battle to protect Earth, just makes it even more rewarding. I can do this.

Cai gives the command to break formation and swoop into the fight. Ri banks to the left and I see a portal open a few feet above and to the side of us. Ri flies towards it as I cast out my magic and close it. But I'm a hairsbreadth too late. A tylwyth squeezes through. It plummets towards the earth, and Ri dives after it. The sudden movement flips my stomach over, but I don't let it distract me.

I have a good line of sight and we are close enough, so I send out a blast of magic and disintegrate the tylwyth. Ri swoops back up, towards where the portals are opening. I feel numb. The only other thing I've ever killed is a squirrel that I hit accidentally with my car. Maybe I'll freak out later, but right now I'm fine. In fact, I'm more than fine, I'm eager to do it all again. I'm scanning the sky, looking for signs of another portal opening and the only thing I feel is a zealous need.

I spy one and urge Ri towards it. He cuts through the air gracefully and I close the portal before anything gets through. A triumphant whoop of glee escapes me just as we glide past Je. Cai looks even more formidable than ever with his goggles and mask on but he gives me a thumbs up. The gesture fills me with dizzying pride.

Ri banks hard, and I realise he has seen another portal. I summon my magic and surrender myself to the rhythm of the battle. Swoop, bank, dive, fly. Close a portal. Chase an invader and blast it. Repeat.

The night is filled with the beat of dragon wings and the sizzle of magic and the determined cries of riders. The tylwyth are eerily silent and they don't fight back. They just try to get past our defence. Their behaviour unsettles me. It stirs something buried deep within, a thought that is just out of reach, like a memory I just can't grasp. But I dismiss it. Of course their behaviour is odd. They are alien demon fairy things. They are hardly going to act like beings from this realm.

"Kirby, Harlen. Five have got through. Pursue!" orders Cai, through my earpiece.

Ri folds his wings and we fall into a dive. The tylwyth are ahead of us, it's going to be hard to catch up with them, gravity likes things to fall at the same speed, so it's going to be against us. Zh and Je join the dizzying race to the ground. Dragons can shape themselves in a way that is more streamlined than the lanky tylwyth, so hopefully wind resistance will slow them down, but it's going to be damn close.

They are too far away to disintegrate with a blast of raw power, but I have a heart stopping spell that works at a fair distance. I'm probably close enough for that. But do tylwyth have hearts? Only one way to find out.

I close my eyes and reach out with my magic. There is a beating heart in the invader's chest. It's startlingly similar to a human one. This is great, I can squeeze it and make it stop. But wait, there is something else here. Something that connects the creature to its comrades. A hive mind? Whatever it is, I think I can still this one's heart and send a blast out that will cease the hearts of the closest tylwyths at the same time. There is nothing to lose by trying.

I open my eyes and see the five tylwyths falling, sprawled and lifeless through the sky. A wave of Ri's impressed astonishment washes through me.

"How the hell did you do that?" barks Cai in my earpiece.

"It's hard to explain," I say.

"When we get back to the castle you are going to explain in minute detail!"

"Yes, sir!" I grumble.

Riders are extremely informal, in my opinion. There really is no expectation for me to call Cai sir, but he is pissing me off. Can't he be happy for me? Proud? Pleased?

He really doesn't need to act as if I've done something wrong.

Zh swoops into position next to Ri and Harlen gives me a big double thumbs up. Cai would kill him for talking unnecessarily over the comms, so I really appreciate the gesture. At least someone is proud of me.

A quick glance around confirms that there are no more portals and no more tylwyth. I guess we will stick around until Cai decides the attack really is over. But it looks like we are done for tonight. No one is hurt. No invaders got through. I call that a success.

It's a shame I won't be returning to a celebration, instead of a grilling from Cai. But maybe he won't interrogate me for long and I'll be able to escape and celebrate with Harlen, Tegwyn, Dai and the others. And I know Natasha and Rowan will be keen to congratulate me on my first fight.

So if Cai goes easy on me, it will all be good.

I can only hope.

Chapter Twenty-One

I'm going to drop this box of tools if Rowan keeps making me laugh like this. Her hilariously recounted tale of her disastrous date is going to have me helpless on the floor in a minute. We are supposed to be carrying tools out to the garden, not laughing hysterically in the hallway.

"There you are!" calls Dai as he jogs up to me.

I wipe tears out of my eyes with the crook of my elbow. "Yeah?"

"Flight Commander wants to see you in his office."

I groan in dismay. Cai grilled me for hours last night right after the battle. I'm dismayed that he is already keen for round two. I told him everything I know, I explained my spell and the hive mind connection thing that I found, but it seems he wasn't content with any of my answers. Fuck my life.

I thrust my box of tools at Dai, hard enough to make him grunt and stagger back a step. Shooting the messenger isn't fair, but hey, it's satisfying.

"Guess I'll catch you later," I say to Rowan and Natasha as I walk away.

"Good luck!" calls Natasha with a pitying look in her eyes.

I'm starting to get the impression that everyone else in the castle is far more frightened of Cai than I ever was. On one hand, I like that. It makes me feel that there has always been a connection between us, that I understand him on a deeper level than other people do. On the other hand, it could just show that I'm a shit judge of character and that maybe Cai has all the red flags and I should stay the hell away from him.

It's an unsettling thought. Not the least because I'm pretty sure it is far too late to stay away from Cai. I'm already in too deep and I don't possess that kind of willpower.

Maybe Harlen will be the buffer. Everyone likes him. And if he is madly in love with Cai, Cai can't be that bad, can he?

I sigh and knock on Cai's office door.

"Enter!" calls a voice that is not Cai's.

Curiosity chases all my other thoughts away. I open the door and step inside. An older man is sitting at Cai's desk. His pale hair is cut very short and his ice blue eyes seem as if they are trying to pierce through my soul. His dark suit looks expensive and severe.

My gaze flicks to Cai, who is standing behind the stranger with his arms crossed. Cai's hair is tied back in a neat tail and he is wearing a suit of all things.

My gaze flicks back to the older man. They have the exact same cheekbones.

"Are you Cai's dad?" I ask in surprise.

The stranger frowns. "I am Morwyn Mordred. Mordecai's father."

Well, fuck this guy. Those six words he just spoke tell me everything I need to know about him and say an awful lot about Cai's childhood. In fact, those six words have just explained so much about Cai. Jeez. As soon as I get Cai alone, I'm giving him a giant hug whether he likes it or not.

"Sit!" says Cai's dad, and it's definitely an order and not an invitation.

I lower myself into the chair facing the desk and try not to glower. I don't think I've ever instantly hated someone so much. I'm going to think of him as Cai's dad, precisely because he doesn't like it, and I am that petty and spiteful.

"Explain how you killed five tylwyths at once," snaps Cai's dad.

For fuck's sake. Why is everyone acting like it is such a big deal? It wasn't that hard or complicated. Unease is making me feel itchy. I assume Cai's dad is high ranking in Dragonrider society and he has been sent to investigate me, which seems over the top. What am I missing?

I swallow over my dry throat and calmly explain what I did, as clearly as possible. When I finish, Cai's dad is still scowling and Cai's expression is carefully blank.

"If you were able to meld with the tylwyth so well, they could have seen inside you too. They could be lurking in there now, waiting to use you."

I stare at him in horror. That is a ridiculous notion. I didn't sense their thoughts at all. I merely was able to discern that their hearts were connected. I'm not some sort of spy or infiltrator.

But this is a man who believes with his whole heart that what you like in the bedroom affects your status as a man. And not only believes it, but preaches it to his child. So clearly his grip on reality is flimsy.

Cai's dad jumps to his feet, sending his chair screeching across the floorboards behind him.

"I'm going to have to delve into your mind to verify your version of events."

Well, that's shit. But if it proves my innocence and shuts this asshole up, it will be worth it. I can cope with a bit of discomfort, I'm not that much of a coward.

He strides around the desk and stalks towards me. My hands grab the arms of the chair I am sitting on, and grip tightly. He takes up position behind me. I close my eyes. Cold fingers place themselves on my temples and I grimace.

Blinding pain blasts through me. He is forcing himself into my mind roughly and carelessly. Rummaging through my memories as if they are a drawer of printed photographs. He tosses them aside, crumples others. He picks up one of me railing his son on the full moon, I snatch it back from him before he has a chance to have a proper look at it. But I think he saw too much.

He finds the memories of the battle and dives into them. Twisting them, turning them. Oozing like thick oil through them. I'm going to be sick. He plays the moment I killed the tylwyth, over and over again. Then he dives deeper into my mind. It hurts. He is hunting for any sign of tylwyth, but he is clawing and shredding my consciousness as he does so. I think I'm screaming.

"I said stop!" Cai's voice is cold and deadly.

The pain retreats and I'm alone in my own mind again. I'm aware of Ri, frantic and concerned. Shit. He was always there, observing my mind being pillaged, but the asshole had cut me off from him. I reassure Ri that I'm fine now and tentatively open my eyes.

Cai and his father are glaring at each other while standing nearly toe to toe.

"You didn't find any trace of tylwyth, so leave him alone," says Cai.

His father bristles. "I need to finish my examination to be sure and then I need to take him back with me so other members of the senedd can verify."

"You are not taking him anywhere."

"I am a senedd member and I am your father. You will do as you are told."

Fury flashes in Cai's sapphire eyes. "This is my fortress, my flight, my command. Kirby is one of my riders and he is going nowhere."

Morwyn draws himself up to his full height, which I am delighted to see is not as tall as Cai.

"How dare you!" he snarls.

"I do dare. Now get out of my castle." Cai's eyes are colder than ice, his expression set in stone. He looks stern, unyielding and formidable. I might just fall into a swoon.

"Tegwyn, kindly escort Mr Mordred off of the premises," Cai adds ruthlessly.

Poor Tegwyn opens the door and steps in, looking paler than a ghost. Morwyn bristles once more and then abruptly turns on his heels and storms out, nearly knocking the unfortunate Tegwyn over. Tegwyn regains his balance and then hurries after the angry man, and just like that I'm alone with Cai.

I stumble the three steps it takes to reach him and then I throw my arms around him and bury my face into his chest. He saved me. He stood up to his vile father to save me. His arms wrap around me and I tighten my grip. He is trembling violently.

"Ri! Tell Zh that we need Harlen."

Cai thinks he needs to take care of me, but right now he needs someone to take care of him. Someone strong, someone dominant. Someone who he will believe when they tell him that everything is going to be alright.

My mind is a little sore from being violated, but Cai just found the courage to face his father. The man who is supposed to love and protect him, but I'm pretty sure has only bullied and tormented. Today was uncomfortable for me, but life changing for Cai. A moment that everything pivoted and changed forever.

Harlen runs in, and right up to us without the slightest hesitation. He presses himself up against Cai's back and wraps his arms around both of us.

"Hey Brat," he says softly. "It's alright, I've got you."

Cai sags back against him, and I can feel the tension leaving his body. He stops trembling and I smile in relief. The three of us are standing in the middle of Cai's office, tangled in an embrace and it feels right. It feels like the three of us can face anything. As long as we face it together.

Chapter Twenty-Two

The fact that all my worldly possessions, apart from my car, fit into three cardboard boxes is a bit depressing, but I can't deny that it is also convenient. Taking this trip from my tiny room to the apartment in the north wing of the castle is exhausting enough. Having to do it more than three times would probably kill me. As embarrassing as that is. I really need to start working out more, or you know, at all. Since apparently the enforced rugby playing isn't doing enough.

Hopefully, I can get this last box in before Cai sees how red and sweaty I am. Panting like a steam train isn't exactly a romantic start to living together. Not that we are going to be living together in a romantic way. He wants to keep a close eye on me and he is willing to take up the apartment that comes with being flight commander, just so he can do so.

It's sweet that he is so concerned and protective of me, but I am worried about how much his dad has rattled him. Of course, I'd love to pretend that Cai has secret romantic reasons for wanting us to move in together, and this whole keeping me safe thing is just an excuse.

It's a nice little fantasy. Sod it. I'm going to keep it. It makes me happy, so why not?

As I shove the door to the apartment open with my shoulder, I spy Cai putting plates away in the kitchenette. He is wearing grey sweatpants and a tight white tee shirt, because clearly he is trying to kill me.

I manage to scoot down the hallway to the bedrooms before he turns around. I make it to my new bedroom and dump my box on the floor. That was close! Time for some deep breaths and maybe splashing some water on my face so it returns to a more normal colour.

I hear Harlen walk into the apartment. I can recognise the rhythm of his footsteps.

"Sweet shag pad!" he drawls.

Yep, that is definitely Harlen. I drift down to the open plan living area and kitchenette because I just need to see Cai's reaction. To my immense disappointment, he is merely ignoring Harlen and continuing to put things away in the cupboard.

Harlen grins at me and gives me one of his filthy winks. He is slouching with his hands shoved deep into his jean pockets. The casual, relaxed pose looks great on him. But then again, everything does. He just rolls out of bed oozing sex appeal.

"I'm a little jealous that Kirby is the one that got you to finally accept this lush flat. All your, 'I'm just another rider', stuff was bullshit."

"Fuck off Harlen," mutters Cai.

Harlen walks over and places his hands on Cai's shoulders and starts kneading them. Cai stiffens and freezes but says nothing. He doesn't turn around or step away.

"Cai, you are so tense. If I was a good person, I'd offer you a massage, but I'm not. So how about we fuck Kirby instead?"

What the...? I can feel my mouth hanging open but there is not a thing I can do about it. Cai has turned around and they are both staring at me like a pair of predators. It seems that he likes Harlen's idea.

It's not the full moon. We are not drunk. It's the middle of the day. I'm a bit sweaty from lugging boxes around. Are they seriously just casually suggesting sex like this? I wasn't even sure they saw me that way. I mean, I know they aren't exactly proposing marriage, but I'm still giddy with excitement that they want to take this step.

"Are you going to say no?" teases Harlen with an evil gleam in his eyes.

I'm sure I would be blushing if every single drop of blood in my body hadn't just run to my cock. My stomach is churning, my heart is racing and my head is spinning. How much is excitement and how much is lack of blood flow, I'll never know. Apparently I am completely on board with this.

"Get naked and lie on your back on the table," says Harlen.

My eyes start to bug out. That sounds super kinky. And a little reckless. Though, the dining table does look sturdy enough. I guess the old saying of 'in for a penny, in for a pound,' applies, because the thought of lying naked on the dining table is not giving me second thoughts at all.

Who knew I was so adventurous? But then again, it's probably just pure horniness that is making me so brave and willing. The things people will do to get laid, never ceases to astound me. Guess I'm people now.

My fingers find the hem of my tee shirt. Wait. Am I supposed to make this sexy? Because I sure as hell don't know how to strip tease.

I pull my top off slowly and confidently. That's going to have to do. I'm not brave enough to look at them, but I can feel their eyes on me. Pulling my jeans and boxers down and stepping out of them doesn't feel alluring at all, but hey, now I'm naked.

"Cai, I'm feeling generous. Do you want his ass or his mouth?"

"Ass," answers Cai without a moment's hesitation.

A thin reedy sound escapes out of my throat. It's a horrible, hungry noise. To try to hide it, I move over to the table and start lying down.

"No, sideways, so your head is dangling off the edge," says Harlen.

Dear lord, I'm going to die. Obediently, I swivel around. Harlen takes his place by my head and Cai between my spread legs. They are both still fully dressed and for some reason that is hotter than hell.

"Maybe we should start making him wear a butt plug at all times, so he is always ready for us?" says Harlen conversationally.

Cai makes a noise of disdain. "He needs to be able to ride a dragon."

"Oh, poor Cai. Is that why you are so bad tempered all the time? Having to ride Je while your ass is sore from me?"

"Go to hell," snaps Cai but there is no heat in it.

Harlen chuckles and then feeds me his enormous cock. I splutter and struggle to take it, then Cai's lubed fingers start toying with my hole. Where the hell did the lube come from? Was he hiding it in his sweatpants? Sensations wash over me, deleting all my thoughts. I groan deeply and Harlen seizes the moment to work his cock in deeper. Oh, my god. I'm going to die. This is bliss.

The weight of Harlen's cock in my mouth is divine. His manly scent is flooding my nose. The salty taste of him is sliding over my tongue. I suck on him and he gets even harder. I'm so busy worshipping the cock in my mouth, I barely register what is happening to my ass, but regular jolts of pleasure shoot up from there.

I hear the rip of a condom packet and then my legs are being thrown over Cai's shoulders. With my head dangling down, I feel so wanton, so decadent. I don't feel like I'm being used. I feel revered. The very centre of attention. Two wonderful men are working hard to drive me so wild with pleasure that I lose my mind. And they are succeeding.

As Cai starts to stretch and fill my ass, I moan in delight around Harlen's cock. Harlen groans in appreciation. I guess the reverberations felt good.

Dimly I'm aware of Ri's approval as he stirs from his sleep and walks through the burrow to snuggle up to Je.

Cai starts thrusting in and out of me, hitting my prostate every single time. The surge of sensation makes me wail helplessly around Harlen's cock. I'm already teetering on the very edge of cumming, all my nerve endings are rubbed raw and tingling. My balls are tight and aching. It's ecstasy and torture all at once.

Cai grunts and I feel a gush of warmth through the condom. Suddenly my mouth is empty. Then my ass is too. I'm about to whimper in protest when Cai appears by my head and offers me his soft and now condom free cock. So that was what the condom was for!

I suck him into my mouth eagerly. He gasps. I swirl my tongue over and over his warm, pliant length. He is twitching in a valiant effort to get hard again and I love that I can torment him like this.

Harlen is pushing into me, and my hole is burning in protest. I don't mind, I know how good it is going to feel once it is in. He works his way in slowly. Forcing my body to open up for him. The sensation is intense, and it is hard to remember to keep sucking Cai's cock.

Cai doesn't seem to mind. His slender hands run over my shoulders and start caressing my nipples. I squeak and squirm at the added stimulation.

"So responsive," whispers Cai.

Oh god. Oh god. Oh god. I'm going to blow. Any second now. My entire body is tingling and alight with it. I'm going to scream. I'm going to shoot the biggest load the world has ever seen. It's going to melt my brain and I'm never going to be the same again.

Harlen eases in his last inch, but before I can adjust to that, he starts rocking his hips and stroking my cock with feather soft fingers. A maddening, teasing, taunting, far too soft touch. My back is arching. I'm making all sorts of obscene noises around Cai's hardening cock. My nipples are being tweaked, twisted and rolled. Arousal, lust and mind numbing pleasure is burning through me.

My orgasm builds and builds and builds. Now it is pouring out of me. I'm clenching and writhing and screaming but neither of them stop and the pleasure keeps rolling on and on and on. Everything is far too sensitive. Everything is dancing that line between pain and pleasure.

"Cai, tomorrow, you are going to be the one on the table," growls Harlen.

Cai whimpers and thrusts and suddenly my mouth is flooding with cum and I'm nearly choking on it.

Harlen thrusts deeply and holds still. His hands are gripping my hips now. Holding me flush to him. He grunts and I feel his enormous cock throb a split second before warm wetness bathes my insides.

My mouth is free from cock and cum, so I gasp in some much needed oxygen. Harlen manoeuvres me so I'm lying lengthwise on the table and my head is resting on the wood and no longer dangling upside down. It might help with the dizziness, but I don't think it's going to make that much difference. I close my eyes and wait for reality to reform.

"You still look stressed, Cai. You need to be fucked."

"No! I'm fine. And you just came."

Harlen lets out an evil chuckle. "I only need a minute."

"No."

I hear sounds of movement and what sounds like a scuffle. What the hell is going on? I open my eyes and sit up.

Harlen has Cai bent over the kitchen island. Cai is struggling but Harlen has his arm twisted behind his back in a very secure hold.

"Harlen!" I yell in shocked outrage.

He looks over his shoulder at me. His brown eyes are wide and dark with lust.

"Colour check, Brat," he says to Cai, with a little shove and without taking his eyes off of me.

"Green," gasps Cai.

I feel my brows furrow in confusion. I don't understand what is happening.

"Green means all good, Yellow means I'm not sure, and red means stop," explains Harlen.

I stare at him blankly for a long moment while my mind tries to compute what it just heard.

"You're pretending? This is just a game?" I ask as I gesture at Cai being held down on the counter. I can feel rage building within me. Several times, Harlen's behaviour towards Cai has unsettled me. I'd been frightened, concerned, and they were just acting the whole time?

"Not really," says Harlen. "Cai fights himself and me over what he needs. He needs me to take control. The colour system helps me to know if I'm pushing him too far."

I blink. Okay, that actually makes sense. I'm not a complete idiot, I knew there was a kinky edge to their situationship. But I know nothing about that lifestyle and that makes me feel so clueless, so naïve. I think the word for it is vanilla? But I'm definitely curious. If they are willing to teach me, I'm willing to learn.

"Kirby, why don't you come kneel here and eat Cai's ass to prepare him for me?"

The noise Cai makes goes straight to my spent cock. Okay, I'm really starting to get this. I appreciate the careful way Harlen phrased it as a suggestion, given how much I was freaking out just a moment ago, but if he had ordered me to do it, like he had with telling me to get on the furniture...man that would have been hot.

I scramble off the table. Harlen grins at me and yanks Cai's grey sweatpants down. I fall to my knees at the sight of that glorious ass. It truly is a sight to behold. A thing of beauty and perfection. I edge closer. I've never eaten ass before, but a warm wet tongue in and around your hole is going to feel wonderful. I'm reasonably confident it is a pretty impossible thing to get wrong.

Harlen shoves Cai's legs wider apart with his foot. I take two handfuls of juicy goodness and spread them apart. My tongue gives its first tentative lick of Cai's pink and puckered hole. He gasps. I grin in delight and get to work.

I lick, I flick, I poke, I tease. I slobber and devour. He tastes good and I can't get enough of it. The way his hole flutters and clenches, is driving me wild. His soft moans and gasps are music to my ears. I'm so proud of the pleasure I can give him.

Suddenly, Harlen's hand is on my shoulder, pulling me away. I squawk in indignation. Not that he pays me any heed. He steps into the spot I was just kneeling in and lines up his huge cock. I'm sitting here with my bare ass on the floor, but I have a front row seat and I'm not moving anywhere. I'm drinking in the sight of Harlen sinking into Cai.

The look of rapture on Harlen's face is exquisite. The noises Cai is making are divine. He is overwhelmed, struggling, his body fighting the invasion and I know exactly how it feels. Then he groans. A long, low deep groan that sounds almost like pain and Harlen sinks all the way in. He has breached Cai and made his body surrender.

Harlen rolls his hips and Cai wails. I watch, utterly transfixed. My hand drifts down to my cock and I'm kind of surprised it is hard again already, given how very hard I came earlier. But given my current view, I think even an eunuch would get an erection.

Cai's legs start to tremble. His soft cries are beautiful. I stroke my cock in rhythm with Harlen's thrusts. The air is filled with the sound of slapping flesh, of moans and grunts and ecstatic pleasure.

My balls are already lifting. I'm about to blow and it is going to be wonderful.

Cai's back arches, and a wailing, gasping keen pours out of him. Harlen roars in triumph, his face twisted in sheer bliss. I moan as I peak. Cum shooting out of me and dribbling all over my fingers.

We came together. All three of us at once. I call that a miracle. A very horny, depraved miracle. And there is only one thing I want to know.

When can we do it again?

Chapter Twenty-Three

The pots are bubbling away and the sight, sound and smell is making me unbelievably happy. It's just pasta, because I can't really cook anything else, but I know it will taste good, and I'm cooking it for my…boyfriends? Lovers? I have no idea what we are and I'm not sure I want to be the one to bring up 'that' conversation.

I'm deliriously happy, whatever label fits us best. It really doesn't matter what we call it. Just as long as it continues. Hopefully forever.

Harlen walks into the apartment and comes up to me. He gives me a soft kiss on the top of my head and I nearly melt.

"Can you finish setting the table?" I ask.

"Sure," he agrees easily.

It is really hard not to think about how we used the table yesterday, but I'm damn well going to fight it. I've given the thing a bloody good scrub down and it's all fine.

Whilst I'm fighting off that mental image. Another one sneaks up on me. Cai bent over the island, with Harlen still inside him, and Harlen saying, "So do I get the third bedroom?"

Very underhand, if you ask me. But it worked, Cai agreed. So I'm not complaining about the ethics too much. The three of us living together is going to be wonderful.

Cai strolls in just as I'm dishing up. He takes a seat and eyes the food warily. My heart sinks. It can't look bad, surely? I mean pasta looks like pasta.

"I can't do this every evening," he says.

Harlen sighs, "Yeah, yeah. The flight commander should eat in the scoff hall with his flight."

I hide my sigh of relief. My cooking isn't the problem, Cai's sense of duty is.

"Now and then will be fine, Cai. So just enjoy it."

Cai takes a deep breath and picks up his fork. "You are right. This looks delicious. Thank you, Kirby."

If I smile any wider, my face is going to split. Who knew I was such a slut for approval? I quickly take my seat and start tucking in. It's not bad at all. Though, I'm so happy to be having dinner with just the three of us in our new home that anything would taste great.

My phone pings, and I glance at it. The notification flashes across my screen and makes me smile.

"Who was that?" asks Cai and his blue eyes look fierce.

"Just an acquaintance asking how my new job is going."

Cai frowns at me.

"I haven't told him anything!" I protest. "I wouldn't do that." Does he really have such a low opinion of me? They told me that dragons needed to be kept secret, so I have honoured that.

Cai glares at me for several long heartbeats but then he turns his attention back to his dinner. I glance over at Harlen, who gives me a warm, sympathetic smile.

"Why is it all such a secret anyway? Surely other mages and paranormals could help?" I dare to ask.

We keep the world of magic and non-human's hidden from mundane society and have done so for hundreds of years. One more secret wouldn't be a problem at all.

Cai makes a noise of disgust. "Because people are stupid."

"There is a whole faction of mages who are religiously fanatical about trying to bring the fey back. Who knows what they would think about tylwyth," adds Harlen.

"They'd think they are angels, like idiots in the middle ages," says Cai.

I blink in surprise. Angels? I suppose they do have white feathered wings. I can see how people could make that mistake. I wonder if this is where all the falling angel stories come from. It's an interesting idea. And even if that interpretation is true, the whole angel thing fits Harlen's assertion that tylwyth are beings from somewhere else.

The possibility that they might be angels, doesn't change my feelings about them. Whatever they are, and wherever they are from, it's clear they are a threat. It's unsettling to realise that not everyone would see that.

"And people would hunt dragons to extinction, like they nearly did before," adds Cai.

Okay, Cai really has a low opinion of people. Not that he is wrong. People do generally suck. Big time. I know that all too well. And the thought of Ri being hunted and murdered is horrific. I wonder if he was alive in those times? Did he lose family? I know he is old, but I don't know exactly how old. And asking someone if their family and friends were slaughtered, doesn't seem like a nice topic of conversation to bring up.

"Okay, I get it. It needs to stay a secret," I say.

We eat in silence for a while. The gentle clang of forks against plates is the only sound. I like this easy companionship, this simple domesticity. I could get used to this and I really hope I get the chance to.

As the silence stretches, my stomach starts to twist, and no, it's not my cooking. It's that I'm alone with Cai and Harlen and they are both fairly relaxed. It's a good moment to get to the bottom of what the hell is going on and discover why everyone is freaking out over the fact I killed five tylwyth. Moving in with Cai and Harlen and having mind-blowing sex may have distracted me for a while, but I haven't forgotten the drama my action caused.

But I don't want to ruin this moment and I'm not sure I want to know. It's probably not good news or at least nothing pleasant. And don't they say that ignorance is bliss? That sounds pretty good to me. I'll take the bliss please, thank you very much. Except my damn curiosity won't let me.

I take a deep breath. I need to know. I can't avoid it.

"Um, so what's the big deal about me killing the tylwyth?" I try to say casually.

Harlen and Cai look at each other, their forks frozen half-way to their mouths. Great. That's not a good sign. The moment stretches uncomfortably. It's Harlen who finally speaks.

"Only the Ddewiswyd has ever been able to do that," he says solemnly.

I stare at him. "The what now?"

"The chosen," he explains. "The greatest rider who ever lived. Everyone hopes he will be reincarnated one day."

My shocked gaze flicks between Harlen and Cai but they both look solemn and deadly serious. If this is a prank, it is a damn good one. But this cannot really be happening.

My fork clangs onto my plate. "You seriously think I might be the reincarnation of the chosen one?"

They say nothing. They don't even move. But their silence says everything. My body feels too hot and too cold. Ri grumbles at me sleepily to calm down. Like that is even remotely possible.

"That's the most ridiculous thing I've ever heard," I say into the deafening silence.

I'm not sure they are even breathing now. They are just staring at me. Well, if they expect me to jump up and walk on water or something, they've got a long bloody wait coming.

"Why was your dad so pissy then?" I exclaim. If I'm some chosen one, his reaction doesn't make any sense.

Cai winces, and it is Harlen that answers.

"Because the senedd is only supposed to rule until the Ddewiswyd returns. Power corrupts and they want to keep it."

Fuck. That does make a whole heap of sense. It's actually more believable than everyone falling to their knees and worshipping me. The problem is, I don't want this to be believable, at all. This whole conversation has to be a hallucination. For some reason I get to my feet. I've lost control of my body as well as my grip on reality.

"So this Dewi-whatsit is like some once and future king?" I ask.

They both nod, as if they can't hear how utterly ridiculous this all sounds. I throw my hands up in exasperation.

"I'm not some bloody Jesus King Arthur!"

Harlen laughs, and the sound makes me feel better. Cai holds my gaze for a heartbeat longer before looking away. I can't tell what he is thinking. I can't cope with this. It is all far too much. I storm away towards my bedroom.

"Leave him," says Harlen behind me.

Cai was going to follow me? That makes me feel all warm and gooey inside, despite all the other overwhelming emotions storming through me. But Harlen is right. Right now, I need to be alone.

I have an awful lot to think about.

Chapter Twenty-Four

This high up the air is so fresh it's addictive. I keep wanting to gulp it down. Breathing it in feels cleansing and exhilarating. Far below us the sea gently swells. Above us a thousand stars shine. They seem so close, I swear I could reach out and scatter them, maybe even pluck one and keep it.

I know some of the others are amused by my exuberance, but fuck them, if I ever start to take this for granted, shoot me.

Je swoops beside us. Cai's goggles are on the top of his head and his mask is tucked under his chin. He is grinning at me. I grin back. He gets it. Out here nothing else matters. There is only sky. Sky, stars, sea and freedom. Dragons are wonderful company. I could live out here forever. A raw fish diet would be worth it.

"I like sleeping in my warm dark burrow."

I laugh. Of course Ri wouldn't want to fly all the time. He can be so literal sometimes.

"Of course," I reassure him. *"And I couldn't exactly be on your back for a full moon, could I?"*

Ri laughs in agreement and swoops down in a dizzying twist. We are on patrol but apparently we still get to have fun. As long as we don't tire ourselves out and remain ready to fight.

Je and Zh give chase and I whoop with joy. Tegwyn and Dai and their dragons Si and La keep pace with us but don't dive. They were happy to play earlier, so I don't think they disapprove.

Ri soars back up, Zh and Je hot on his tail. This is wonderful. I know Cai and Harlen are not supposed to be on patrol at the same time. It's too dangerous. As first and second in command, the risk of losing them both is a tactical disaster. They are bending the rules because they feel like they need to keep me safe. I don't think they suspect Tegwyn and Dai specifically, it's more that they don't know who might be working for the senedd.

I feel my mood start to plummet. So I firmly steer my thoughts away from that path. They didn't ground me, and now we are all flying together. It's all good. Everything is great.

Everyone will come to their senses soon enough and realise that I'm not the chosen one. Sanity will resume. And life will carry on.

"I chose you. You are my chosen one."

"Thank you Ri. That's very sweet of you."

A cold shiver runs down my spine, one that has nothing to do with Ri's words. All my senses fire up to high alert. I'm sitting ramrod straight on Ri's back and I have no idea why. Dread is coiling in my stomach. A sense of impending doom is suffocating me.

I send a mental image to Ri of the patch of sky we need to be in.

"Where are you going?" asks Cai in my earpiece.

"Portals," I say robotically. "Portals about to open. Many, many of them."

Cai swears. "I can't see or sense anything."

"We have less than five minutes," I snap. "Sound the alarm."

Nobody can tell when a portal is about to open. That's not how they work. Wards and sigils can give a few moments notice if they are set correctly. If you are very attuned, you might get a few seconds or possibly a minute. But I can feel these ones coming and I've never been more sure of anything in my life.

The others are following me now. I hear the beeping in my ear that signifies Cai has triggered the sirens. The rest of the flight will be here soon. Good, we are going to need them.

"Are you sure?" Harlen asks Cai.

"It will be a good drill, if nothing else," says Cai.

I don't blame them for not believing me. I wouldn't believe me. We are supposed to fly around and be the first to respond when any of the multiple wards sent across the sky are set off. We are not supposed to sense them coming.

We are drawing up to the location I asked Ri to fly to. The ward lights up. Then a sigil wails. We are already here. Because I somehow knew.

A portal opens and then another one and another. The first one is big enough for two tylwyth to dive through. Shit. Containing all this before the rest of the flight gets here is going to be a challenge.

I send out a blast of magic and slam the first portal shut. Ri dives after the tylwyth. The fight is on. The world shrinks until all that exists is the hunt. Ri and I work seamlessly together as one. We fly close enough to the portals to close them. We fall through the sky to catch the invaders who get through. We do it over and over again.

When the rest of the flight arrive, the desperate pace slows down, but it's still intense. There is a rhythm and flow to it though and I feel attuned to it. I've got this. I'm good at this. I let time drift away from me and I lose all sense of it.

Ri rises up from despatching yet another tylwyth. A faint pink glow is painted across the eastern horizon. I can't see any more portals and there are only dragons in the sky.

"Any injuries?" asks Cai.

Like everyone else, I dutifully check myself and Ri over. There is not a scratch on either of us. Not that I can see or feel anyway. Apart from being a little out of breath and a little drained of magic. I'm none the worse for wear.

Cai gives the order to return home and the dragons swoop and bank into formation. As we fly, the sun starts peeking over the sea, turning it pink and gold.

I hear a click in my earpiece that signifies a private channel. "Are you really alright?" asks Harlen, risking Cai's wrath to talk to me. Comms are not for idle chatter.

"I'm fine, why?"

"You closed a shit load of portals and killed an insane amount of tylwyth."

Harlen sounds super impressed. A little awed even. I don't think I did anything that impressive. He is being weird. All this Ddewiswyd nonsense has gone to his head.

"Still not the chosen one," I say with gritted teeth.

Harlen chuckles. "If you say so."

His tone very much implies that he doesn't believe me. I look around and see other riders casting odd glances my way. Though I could just be being paranoid. It is hard to read peoples' expressions from dragon back, they are just too far away. But they are definitely turning their heads to look at me.

A sick, uneasy feeling settles in my stomach. Cold, stark realisation strikes me and it is as startling as it is awful.

There is not much difference between being the chosen one and everyone believing that you are.

I shudder. Well shit. Now what the fuck am I supposed to do?

Chapter Twenty-Five

The television is mostly playing to itself. I for sure as hell don't know what's going on, I think it is a property renovation show. Whatever it is, it makes a comforting background noise, and it's something to stare blankly at.

The sofa in the apartment isn't very comfy, so it's a good thing I'm leaning on Harlen, with my legs on Cai's lap. I had fully expected to be thoroughly grilled as soon as we got back at dawn, but they have both been strangely quiet. We grabbed a few hours of sleep and now we are vegging out in front of daytime TV.

I don't really want to think about what happened last night, or the implications of it. Being good at closing portals and dispatching tylwyth is something I can dismiss. Sensing that portals were about to open, is far harder to ignore.

I don't want to be the chosen one. And I really don't want people to make me the chosen one just because they have decided to believe that it is true. I just want to remain a nobody. An ordinary Dragonrider. Not that there is anything ordinary about riding dragons.

But I have a horrible, sinking feeling that this accusation will not go away if I ignore it. I'm going to have to face it and deal with it somehow. There has to be a way to get people to see sense. I just need to find it.

"Since I'm the chosen one, I think you should make me a cup of tea," I say to Cai.

He dumps my legs off of his lap and strides over to the kitchenette. I stare at him in openmouthed horror. Oh, my fucking god. Cai doesn't truly believe this shit, does he? Even if he does, I don't want him obeying my every word. I can't think of anything worse.

"I was joking!" I wail in dismay.

Cai shrugs while keeping his back to me. "I don't mind making tea for people I like."

"You like me?" I splutter.

I mean I kind of knew he did, but I never thought I'd hear him say it out loud. And it's wonderful enough to fully distract me from all this chosen one nonsense.

"You are good at sucking cock," he says tonelessly.

Well, fuck him. But actually that is flattering. Damn the obnoxious bastard, now I don't know if I should be pissed off or pleased. Why does he always confuse me like this?

"Stop being mean to Kirby or I will spank you," drawls Harlen.

Cai freezes. One hand is on the cupboard door and one hand is holding a box of tea bags midair. His back is ramrod straight. I'm getting the very distinct impression that it is not fear that is freezing him.

Harlen chuckles. A deep sound, full of delight. And since I'm leaning on him, it reverberates right through me. It makes me shiver in delight.

"Okay, how about, stop being mean to Kirby and I will spank you as a reward," says Harlen, his voice deep and low with promise.

Cai bristles and resumes moving. Deftly lining up three mugs by the kettle before shutting the cupboard door with a little bit more force than is necessary.

"You are not spanking me," he mutters. "Ever."

Somehow, I manage to hold in my giggle. He is wrong. Now Harlen knows he wants it, it's going to happen. It's merely a matter of time. And I better bloody be there when it does, or I will be seriously pissed at Harlen.

A few short minutes later, Cai returns to the sofa with the drinks. A tea for me and coffee for him and Harlen. I take a sip. Delicious, just how I like it. Milk with two sugars and fairly weak. Oh gosh. He knows how I like my tea, he didn't even have to ask. Call me super British, but that is a sign of true love.

He likes coffee with a ton of milk and enough sugar that he should have diabetes by now. Harlen likes his coffee black and strong. Oh, my goodness. It is true love. I know their drinks. We are soul mates.

Harlen pulls Cai closer and I nearly spill my tea. He puts his fingers under Cai's chin and makes him look at him.

"It's just us here, Brat. You can let it all go. You don't need to be an asshole."

Then before Cai can say a word, Harlen kisses him. Deeply. Thoroughly. Passionately. I'm inches away and it is a sight to behold. I can see everything. I see Cai tense and resist. I see him waver. I watch him surrender with a soft moan and turn all pliant and soft. By the time Harlen is done with him, Cai is a melted puddle of goo. His eyes are baby blue and hazy. Harlen was right all along. Cai really is adorable once you get to know him.

Harlen turns back to his coffee. Cai sighs contently and rests his head on Harlen's shoulder. The one I'm not leaning on. Then Cai curls his whole body up as close to Harlen and me as he can get. Harlen puts his drink down on the coffee table and then wraps one arm around Cai and the other around me. I feel his chest swell and I can almost taste the pride and sheer joy rolling off of him.

I'm smiling so much that my face is hurting. The three of us together, just works. I don't care that it is unusual or something I never expected. I certainly don't care that some people will disapprove. Our happiness is none of their business. I couldn't choose just one of them and why should I have to? This is perfect.

Except, one thing is niggling at me.

"It will be the full moon soon," I say, trying to keep the anxiety out of my voice.

Cai caresses my leg in a comforting gesture. "Our dragons know how we feel."

"And it will be rubbing off on them," adds Harlen. "The three of them were always close anyway."

I really am going to burst with happiness. Not just from the assurance that the full moon will not be a problem, but from Cai's thinly cloaked confession of feelings. And Harlen's confirmation of them. Dragonriders are apparently terrible at communication, but I love them anyway.

Chapter Twenty-Six

I'm sobbing into this pillow. It's soaked with my tears and drool. Probably snot too. My ass is in the air and Harlen is pounding it. Far, far away, Ri is lying on the dark sand of a deserted beach. Zh is mounting him and biting his neck and Ri is in ecstasy.

I wail as another tidal wave of pleasure consumes me. This full moon feels intense. Everything is just so much...more. I'm lost in Ri's emotions with no hope of untangling myself. And this deep, deep hunger within me is growing. I need to be filled. Stretched. Taken. Possessed. I crave it more than I have ever craved anything. I'm burning up with this thirst.

Harlen gasps. "Ri is going into heat."

"Je can smell it too," says Cai.

Suddenly a straw is poking in my face.

"Drink!" orders Cai.

I open my mouth, catch the straw and obey. The water is cold and delicious. Cai strokes my hair and Harlen continues to thrust into me.

"You need to keep your strength up, Kirby. The longer you can last, the longer Ri can too. It's a feedback loop. And the more seed Ri receives, the higher the chances are that his eggs will take."

Cai's voice is calm. The tone even. But in my heightened state I can hear the notes of his excitement and his anxiety.

"We have to ask Je and Zh to let the other dragons near. They are already circling," Cai says to Harlen.

"Kirby will hate that," grunts Harlen without losing his rhythm. "If he gets upset and stressed, then so will Ri."

Far away on the moonlight beach, Zh spreads her golden wings wide. Warning the other dragons to back off. Ri squirms in delight at the display of possessiveness.

Cai makes a noise of frenzied frustration and dismay. I can almost imagine him hopping from foot to foot. It's strange to see him like this. I can read his conflict, as clear as day. He is desperate for Ri's eggs to take, it's the most important thing in the world to him. But he doesn't want to hurt me.

"I'll make some Yohimbe!" declares Cai.

"Wait!" groans Harlen. "I'm...I'm...you need to take over. I'll make the disgusting tea."

His rhythm gets all jerky and uncoordinated and then with a yell, he spills deep inside me. He pulls out and I scream. Being empty is awful. I'm cold. My body cramps, trying to clench down on what is not there. On the beach, Ri cries out in pain, even though Zh is still filling him.

Cai's cock slides into me, and I sob in sheer relief and joy. He picks up a similar rhythm to Harlen and everything is bearable. Zh finishes and steps aside for Je. Then everything feels wonderful again. It's much better when there is a synchronicity between us and our dragons. Cai's pace slows to longer, shallower thrusts and my human body can't take it. I'm going to cum, but I won't be able to stop being fucked afterwards. I wail and try to hold back my orgasm. I need to keep going. It would be incredible if Ri's eggs took, there haven't been any young for a hundred years. Dragons are still at risk of extinction. I can't let my lack of stamina ruin everything.

But my body is only human. There is only so much stimulation it can take. My orgasm roars through me. Obliterating everything in its path. It floods Ri. My pleasure becomes his pleasure. I feel his body soften in response, open up more and let Je in deeper. Closer to the eggs.

I'm making a difference. I'm helping. My lust and desire is helping.

Cai continues to steadily pump into me. It continues to feel good. More sensitive, yes, but not unbearably so. As my peak recedes, I'm still hungry. Still flooded with desire and arousal. I want this. I want to stay like this all night. My ass in the air, Cai and Harlen taking turns to pump me full of seed.

Fill me until my belly swells with it and my eggs are bathed in it. Okay, that was Ri's thought, not mine. I need to keep some sort of separation. If I can.

"Are you okay?" asks Cai.

"Yes!" I yell. "Don't stop. Don't ever, ever stop," I beg.

"We won't," he promises.

A disgusting smell fills the room. Harlen has returned with the tea. I hear him take a sip and then splutter.

"Oh god that's vile!"

"But it will keep you hard all night," says Cai.

"The things we do for duty," chuckles Harlen.

He is a fine one to talk. He is not the one laying here with their ass in the air begging to be fucked all night. Talk about taking one for the team. Though it's more a very filthy fantasy come to life than a hardship. Especially now I know I can cum and keep going. A night of endless orgasms. Would anyone say no to that?

Cai grunts softly and splashes my insides with his cum. It feels wonderful. It feels like hitting the spot, scratching the itch and getting exactly what I'm craving.

But then he is pulling out of me and I'm shrieking in horror.

"I'm not ready yet, Kirby. You'll have to make do with this until the tea kicks in," says Harlen.

Something slides into my empty hole. Something soft and very warm. It's a dildo, and it has been heated up to mimic the heat of a dragon's cock. A sordid sound of delight and appreciation pours out of me. It feels wonderful. It feels like a caress against the puffy walls of my channel. I groan and whimper and roll my hips back against it.

I can hear Cai and Harlen sipping their tea and it has to be the most surreal moment of my life. I'm here writhing in carnal ecstasy on the bed and two people are standing around drinking tea.

"I'm ready," breathes Harlen.

"No using his mouth or jerking off, or using me. Every drop needs to go in his ass. The more he takes, the more receptive Ri will be," says Cai sternly.

"I know, I know," mutters Harlen.

He pulls the dildo out and I bite my bottom lip in an effort not to scream in dismay. His hands grab my hips and then his huge, wonderful cock is impaling me and everything is right with the world.

On the beach, Ri is wriggling and encouraging Zh to go deeper. He wants to feel as gorged as I am. This feedback thing is really working. I can save a species from extinction by being a horny bastard who loves getting railed.

Laughter bubbles out of me. The movement tightens the muscles in my abdomen and moves Harlen's cock. I groan. That felt strange. And good.

"You okay?" gasps Harlen. I think it felt good for him too.

"Never better," I manage to murmur.

Now it's Harlen's turn to laugh, and that movement pulls a keening noise from me. It's going to be a long, unforgettable night.

Chapter Twenty-Seven

As my consciousness reforms, my thoughts go straight to Ri. Just before I crashed out, he'd been sleeping, sated and exhausted on the beach. Je and Zh were standing guard and I know they were somewhere super remote like Iceland or Greenland or something, and they have cloaking magic, but I can't stand the thought of them exposed and vulnerable like that. Especially now that the sun is up.

I reach out with my mind and find that Ri is home now. Curled up, fast asleep in his burrow under the castle. Je and Zh are still standing guard. They must have flown home while I was out cold.

Satisfied that Ri is safe, my mind turns its attention to my body and I groan. Everything hurts. All my muscles ache and my ass is on fire. Harlen and Cai were careful and used plenty of lube, but there is only so much pounding delicate tissue can take.

I also feel incredibly sticky, as if I'm drenched in sweat and cum. Which, probably isn't too far from the truth.

"How do you feel?"

I open my eyes to find Cai a few inches away. His gaze is aquamarine and full of concern. Harlen's broad warmth is at my back. They'd both been behind me when I had fallen into darkness. We'd been spooning, with me as the littlest spoon. Cai had been inside me and Harlen had been mercilessly milking Cai's prostate with his fingers. Causing Cai to shudder and writhe and spill inside me over and over again. I should really be asking him if he is okay. That must have been exhausting.

"Did it work?" I ask.

"We won't know for a while, probably not until the next full moon. Are you sore?"

I nod and Cai frowns.

"Let's get you into the shower and then I'll get the healer to come and check you over."

My entire body shudders. "No, to the eternal examination, yes to the shower."

Cai's blue eyes narrow but I meet his gaze steadily until he relents. This, 'might be the chosen one' stuff, does have its perks.

"Fine," he grumbles. "Harlen, wake up you giant oaf and carry Kirby to the shower."

"I'm awake, I'm awake," yawns Harlen. "What am I doing?"

"Helping Kirby to the shower," says Cai with gritted teeth.

In the end, they both have to help me into the spray and then Harlen has to hold me up because my legs have turned into wet noodles. The hot water cascading down my aching muscles feels wonderful. Cai squeezes into the shower too and gently soaps my body. Then he turns me around so that I'm standing chest to chest with Harlen, my arms wrapped around his neck. The warm wet manly smell of him is gorgeous. As is the feel of his firm muscles pressing into me.

Cai does a fantastic job of washing my hair. His is fairly long, so it makes sense that he knows what he is doing. I groan in bliss.

Cai drops to his knees behind me and gently spreads my ass cheeks apart. He carefully runs a soft sponge over my hole and I hiss in discomfort. The sponge doesn't return. Cai just kneels there, holding my cheeks apart, letting the warm shower water run down my crack and right over my abused hole. I can only imagine what it looks like.

"Stop being a perv, Cai," teases Harlen.

"Fuck you!" snaps Cai vehemently, but Harlen just chuckles.

Cai gets to his feet and switches the water off. I mumble a drowsy complaint but then I'm being dried and swaddled with fluffy towels and it feels great too.

"My mum is going to be so proud of me," beams Harlen. "Shower assistant to the chosen one."

"Piss off!" I say but with no real heat.

Harlen chuckles again and I can really see why Cai hates him most of the time. He is an annoying, infuriating jerk. But he is not talking complete nonsense. I know I really helped Ri last night. Helping dragons conceive would be seen as a superpower to riders. It is really going to make me look like the chosen one now. For fuck's sake.

Harlen carries me, fully bundled in towels, to the living area and I'm stupidly grateful when he places me on the sofa instead of on one of the hard chairs around the dining table.

Cai thrusts a cup of tea into my hand. It has more sugar in it than I normally like, but it is just what I need. I sigh in contentment and look up at them. They are both standing there, hovering over me. Damp from the shower and with just a towel thrown round their waist. While I very much appreciate the view, they don't need to fuss quite this much.

I wonder if they realise just how much they are mimicking their dragons guarding Ri.

"You do know, I'm not the one who is going to get pregnant?" I ask as I take another sip of tea. "Go dry off properly, get dressed and come have tea too. You worked hard last night as well."

They both hesitate for a moment before hurrying off to do my bidding. They return in record speed, Harlen just in boxers and Cai in grey sweats and a loose white tee shirt.

Harlen makes coffee and they both join me on the sofa. One on either side of me.

I sip my tea and sigh. Are they being this attentive because of their dragons' influence? Or because they think I'm the chosen one? Or because it's just who they are? It's probably a combination of all three, and I should let it go. It's nice, whatever the cause is. I should just relax and enjoy it.

"Please tell me we can have a duvet day?" I ask.

The thought of having to move, let alone ever doing anything ever again, is extremely daunting. I need at least twenty-four hours of vegging out on the sofa. If Cai says we have to work, I think I might actually cry.

"You and Harlen can. I have work to do."

Harlen and I both turn our heads to look at him and he squirms a little under the intensity of our gaze.

"You need to rest too, Brat," rumbles Harlen.

A long tense moment passes. Cai's gaze flicks between me and Harlen and I feel bad for ganging up on him but it is for his own good. He is his own worst enemy.

"I can bring my laptop up from my office and do some work while we watch TV," he concedes.

I smile. I call that a victory. Baby steps towards Cai letting us take care of him. It's a fantastic start and a brilliant foundation to work on.

Everything is working out wonderfully. Our relationship is getting stronger, Ri might bear eggs that will hatch into young. It's all great.

I just need to wriggle out of this chosen one nonsense and everything will be perfect.

Chapter Twenty-Eight

I'm in the castle's main kitchen, slowly chopping my way through a mountain of potatoes when the siren sounds. I shouldn't be so relieved, but I am. I quickly put down my knife and wipe my hands off on a cloth. Seems I prefer battle over chores. There is something seriously wrong with my self-preservation instincts.

"Are you sure you are going to be able to ride?" says Natasha with a wink.

I stick my tongue out at her and head off to the kit room. She's not wrong. It's been two days since the full moon and I'm still a bit dubious about sitting in the saddle. Not that anyone else needs to know about that. They all know far too much as it is. Everyone's dragons knew about Ri going into heat and Zh and Je tag teaming all night, so the riders all guessed what happened to me. And then of course they just had to tell the non-riders.

There is no privacy in a castle full of riders, none at all. But I guess it is a small price to pay for all the upsides.

The kit room is bustling but everyone makes room for me to reach my riding leathers. It feels like parting the sea. Except, the only power here is their belief in me. I could treat it as another perk, but I'm not that stupid. With great power comes great responsibility and all that.

I don't want to be the chosen one. I'm too selfish. I've seen how hard Cai works and any chosen one would have to work even harder. I'm not a natural leader. I like being told what to do, and not just in the bedroom. Orders are comforting. Responsibility is awful.

Chosen ones also get a ton of enemies and often end up martyred. So, yeah, thanks but no thanks.

I hurry over to the tack room. Ri's saddle looks extra shiny. Did someone polish my saddle for me? Holy fuck. This is already getting out of hand. But I haven't got time to deal with it now. I grab my super nice smelling saddle and jog over to Ri.

"Are you sure you want to fight?" I ask him.

He huffs as he lowers his belly to the ground so that I can place the saddle on his back.

"If I am carrying, I'm carrying eggs. I'm not injured or dead."

"Fair enough,"

I quickly put the saddle on him and he stands up so I can run the girth under his belly. I thread it through the buckle and test the tightness. It feels good to me.

"Is it too tight?" I ask.

"Kirby!" snaps Ri. I've never heard him sound so grumpy. *"My belly will not get big like a human's and even if it were, it's far too early. Stop fussing! You are worse than Je and Zh."*

"Okay, okay, I'm sorry. It's awful being nagged, I know. I'll try my best to stop."

Ri rumbles vocally. A low sound that can only just be heard by human ears. He is slightly appeased and is going to think about forgiving me.

I smile and swing myself up onto his back. I wince as I sit but it's more from anticipation than actual discomfort. The reality is bearable. Possibly because of excitement and adrenaline. But, hey it works.

Ri gives a little shake. His eagerness to fight and fly flows through me, inciting my own keenness. I feel positively feral and bloodthirsty.

"Good!" growls Ri.

Cai and Harlen are just finishing with their saddles, so I fiddle with my gloves, goggles and mask. Anything to stop me watching them swing up onto their dragons. I'm learning. Ri chuckles at me and I grin.

Cai gives the signal and as one the flight moves forward. The drop passes swiftly and then we are soaring. Free in the sky. The wind blows away all my troubles until only this moment and the impending fight remains.

Ri stills his dark wings, spreads them wide, tilts sharply to the left and glides into formation with the other dragons. I'm no longer Kirby or even Kirby and Ri. I am a flight of dragons. A tribe of war. Gliding through the night sky on the way to protect Earth while everyone sleeps in their beds, ignorant and happy far below.

An arc of eldritch green Aurora Borealis lights up the night just in front of us. We are nearly there. Excitement is thrumming through my veins. My magic is humming within me in anticipation.

I see a portal start to open. The patrol riders are closer and they are coping well. Cai hasn't given the command to break formation and join the fray, but I want this portal. No one else has seen the shimmer of its approach. I urge Ri towards it.

Seconds later Cai gives the command. Shame flashes through me briefly. He is the flight commander. He knows what he is doing. He deserves my respect, I shouldn't have broken rank. But as Ri swoops closer to the now visible portal, everything else falls away. There is nothing in my soul apart from magic and dragon wings and the pursuit of my prey.

Once again time falls away. The fight is the only thing that exists. This moment could have lasted seconds or millennia. It doesn't matter. Not letting any tylwyth reach Earth is the only thing that does.

Ri banks sharply to the left and suddenly I'm falling. The night sky is screaming past my ears. I stare in astonishment at the saddle falling through the sky, its long frayed girth whipping in the empty air.

Tonight is the night I die? That's unexpected. My stomach cramps cold and distant. My body is scared but my mind is blank.

Ri hurtles past me in a torrent of air and night. Then I'm slamming onto his back, so hard it knocks every breath I've ever had out of me. Pain lances through me. I'm weak and dizzy and sliding off. My stunned body scrabbles at his smooth scales but can't find purchase and then I'm falling again. Ri roars and chases after me. He can't grab me with either teeth or claws, both are far too sharp and riding leathers far too tight. Our leathers really should have long flowing straps attached to them, for occasions like this. If they were colourful ribbons, they'd look pretty fluttering in the wind.

I picture Cai glaring and formidable with bright multicoloured ribbons festooned over his riding leathers and I want to laugh, but I can't get any air into my lungs, it's all rushing past me far too fast.

The air turns damp with brine. Hitting the sea is not going to save me. We were so very high up in the sky. I've fallen so far and so fast, the waves are going to smash me to pieces. At least it will be quick.

A parachute would be better instead of ribbons, some part of my mind informs me. I have to agree with it. I try telling Ri to tell Cai to make parachutes part of the uniform, but I don't know if he has heard me.

A golden light surrounds me. I'm glowing. Am I dead already? Did I miss the moment of impact? No, I'm still falling, but slower than I was. I stare at the gold surrounding me. It's magic. Someone's magic is slowing my fall. What the hell? Telekinesis is mind bogglingly hard. It takes an insane amount of magic. And that's just to move a simple object. Magically fighting gravity over something the size of a human body? I'd say it was impossible if I wasn't seeing it with my own eyes, feeling it with my own body. I can breathe now and the weight of the air is no longer bending my body. The golden magic caresses me, cocoons me. My scattered mind belatedly recognises the feel of it. It's Cai. Cai's essence is all around me, holding me, protecting me, saving me.

Ri swoops under me, and this time when I hit his back it is nowhere near so hard. I can grab his spiny neck ridges and hold on. I've been saved. Ri gives an almighty thrust of his wings and the tips skim the waves, splashing cold sea water on me. That was close, so very close.

It hurts to breathe, I think I have broken ribs. I'm trembling all over but I'm alive.

Zh swoops just above Ri, so close that I can touch her golden scales. Harlen leans down and pulls me up. He sits me in front of him and wraps his arms around me. This is a good idea. Fainting and falling off again would be terrible.

Suddenly, Zh banks so hard to the right that we are vertical. I grab onto the saddle horn and swear. What the fuck? Are they trying to kill me now? I look up, we are under Je, and Cai is falling, his body limp and loose. He falls right into Harlen's arms and my lap.

Straps, we definitely need straps. Straps to tie us to our saddles and straps for dragons to catch when our saddles break. Why has no one ever thought of this before?

Cai looks far too pale. Using that much magic cannot have been good. He looks almost lifeless. Harlen has a good hold of him but I wrap my arms around him too, just in case. If I faint too, I don't know how Harlen will hold both of us. But I know he will.

I look down at Cai's too lifeless face again. He is insanely beautiful to a whole other level when he is not scowling or smirking. Though I'd do anything to see either again. He also looks far younger. Too young to have to deal with all the shit that comes with being flight commander, it's not fair.

"Are you well, Kirby?"

"I will be once we get home and Cai wakes up," I assure him.

And I get someone to heal my ribs. But Ri can probably feel that for himself, there is no need to put it into words.

A wave of tremendous sadness engulfs me. I feel like I'm drowning in it. Then it vanishes. Like a shadow when the light is switched on. I blink. Ri has thrown down some serious mental wards. What is going on? Why is he so sad? I look down at Cai's limp body. He is definitely alive. But does Ri know something? I try to swallow but my throat is too tight.

This isn't good at all.

Chapter Twenty-Nine

I wake up in the infirmary, in a long, narrow and surprisingly comfortable bed. The first thought that flows through me is pride that I stayed conscious until we landed in the stable. The second thought is how nice it is that Harlen is holding my hand. Hot on the heels of that thought, flashes concern for Cai. I scramble up and then breathe a prayer of thanks for whoever has healed my ribs.

Harlen is sitting on a small hard chair facing me. His right hand is holding mine, his left hand is holding Cai's, who is still out cold in the bed next to me. His hair looks golden and stark against the crisp white pillow. He doesn't look as pale as he did earlier but that could just be because we are not under starlight anymore.

"Is he going to be okay?" I ask.

There are dark circles under Harlen's eyes. His face looks drawn and haggard. When his brown eyes meet mine, they are full of grief. He slowly shakes his head. I can feel my heart beat, fast and frantic. The rhythm pulses in my throat.

"He has burnt up all his magic."

My free hand flies up to my mouth but it does nothing to hide my gasp of horror. Cai will never be able to wield magic again. He won't even be able to sense it. He is no longer a mage. It is beyond awful. It is the worst fate I could possibly imagine in my darkest of nightmares.

Below the castle, Ri is trying to comfort a distraught Je. The anguish spills down our connection, so strong that I swear I can taste it on my tongue.

Oh. My. God.

I let out a pained sob. He will never be able to talk to Je again.

Cai can no longer be a dragon rider. He can no longer be flight commander.

He should have just let me die.

"Do not say that!" bellows Ri.

Huge sobs wrack my body. Tears blur my vision and run down my face. Harlen squeezes my hand tighter, but he says nothing. There is nothing to say and we both know it. There are no words for this.

Cai stirs, so I hurriedly scrub the tears off of my face and hold my breath. It's the only way I can hold back my sobs. I need to be strong for Cai, he is the one that needs to fall apart while my strength holds him.

Harlen pulls his chair closer to Cai and releases my hand so he can hold Cai's with both of his. I don't mind at all. It's the right thing to do.

Cai's blue eyes flutter open. He looks at Harlen then searches for me. Relief flashes across his face as our eyes meet. There is no confusion in the sapphire depths of his eyes. No slowly dawning horror. Just pain, torment and sorrow. He knows. I think he knew before he fell off of Je. He felt it, felt his broken, shattered core. Just as Ri did.

I hold his gaze and I can't see any trace of regret. There should be. Burning, twisting and vengeful regret. Bucket loads of it. He should hate and despise me. Loathe my presence. But obscenely he just looks relieved that I'm okay. I guess his sacrifice not being in vain counts for something.

Harlen curls his big frame next to Cai on the narrow infirmary bed. I jump out of mine and shove it up to Cai's so we can all squish up together, making a Cai sandwich. He sighs, closes his eyes and lets us hold him. He is not going to cry, I realise with growing dismay. He is going to hold all that pain and monstrous loss in.

I don't know how to help. I don't know if anyone can.

I take back everything I ever said about not wanting to be the chosen one. If I was the chosen one, I'd be able to fix Cai. I'd have the power to make everything right again. Turn everything back to how it should be.

I close my eyes and pray to whatever deity or fate is watching me. I tell them I accept my destiny, I embrace it. I am willing to do whatever they demand of me. I'll be their puppet, I'll be anything they want me to be. I'll be the chosen one.

Nothing happens. No shining light, no sudden wisdom. No profound power imbues me. I was right all along. I really am not the chosen one. I'm just me. Kirby Taylor. Pathetic and useless. I want to weep again. The disappointment tastes bitter, and to my shame it's laced with relief. My plea to be the chosen one was not wholehearted.

Cai sacrificed everything to save me and apparently I'm too selfish to want to do the same. Dragon riding is everything to Cai, it is his entire world. I've only been a part of this world for a few months and already I know I'd rather die than leave it. This has been Cai's whole life. He was raised to this. Born to it. Thrived in it enough to become flight commander at such a young age.

I'm not a complete idiot and I'm aware that being born into the right family certainly helped a lot. But it wasn't all that. It can't have been. Cai is a brilliant flight commander. Everyone trusts and respects him, which is exactly what you need from your leader. If his dad had just bought him the position, he'd suck at it.

Images flash of his asshole father and further realisation dawns. I bite my bottom lip so hard I taste blood. But it is far better than wailing out loud. Shit. Cai is probably going to lose his family over this too. Morwyn seems just the type to disown his son for this. What good is a son who can't wield magic and has no position? And things have to have been already precarious after Cai threw him out like that.

Cai threw him out to save me. Cai burnt up all his magic and ruined his life to save me.

Oh no. It wasn't to save me. My guts turn to liquid ice. My lungs clamp down and my heart freezes. Stark reality is screaming in my face and I want to scream back into the void. I understand now. I see it as clear as day and I'm utterly appalled and ashamed that I was so oblivious before.

Cai didn't do those things to save me.

He did them to save the chosen one.

Chapter Thirty

It's far too quiet in the apartment when I get out of the shower. Damn it, I wanted to make Harlen breakfast before he left. The poor man looks exhausted and frazzled at being acting flight commander.

Oh well, I can still make Cai breakfast. Last night was his first night of sleeping alone, Harlen and I both hated leaving him, but he insisted it was what he wanted. Well, he has had his night alone in his room. Now I can bring him breakfast in bed.

Maybe I can convince him to go and visit Je again. Though I'm pretty sure he only went yesterday because Ri told me Je hadn't been eating. Je flew out with the other dragons to fish last night, which is great, but leaves me without a reason to coax Cai down to the burrows.

I sigh heavily. Watching Cai tenderly stroke Je's emerald scales while the dragon gently snuffled Cai's hair, had nearly broken me. I had stood there sobbing like a baby and had been incapable of stopping.

The bond between Cai and Je had been strong. The affection between them had always been unmistakable. They truly did seem as one when they were soaring through the sky.

Now I'm thinking about how the only times I've ever seen Cai truly smile have been when he was flying. A wave of utter misery consumes me. Making bacon and eggs feels pointless. They are no compensation for all that he has lost.

Glumly, I finish dressing and make my way to the kitchenette. Breakfast is the only offering I have, so it will have to do. Cai's own resilience and time, are the only things that can heal this. And there is going to be a heck of a scar.

And then it will become obvious that I'm not the chosen one and he will hate me forever.

My breath hitches and I blink back even more stupid tears. I can't fry bacon while crying.

Somehow, I manage to cook a decent breakfast, as well as make a decent cup of coffee. Well, it smells decent. Personally, I think coffee tastes like it has come out of Satan's cock. But each to their own.

I put everything on a tray and walk down the hallway to Cai's room, I shoulder the door open and plaster a bright smile on my face. Then I drop the tray and gasp in horror.

Sunlight is streaming in through the tall windows, catching dancing dust motes. The room is empty. The bed is stripped bare. The shelves and bedside table top are devoid of anything. All the drawers and cupboard doors are neatly shut but I just know they are barren.

I'm running and running. Twisting down stairs, sprinting down hallways. I don't know where my body is taking me, until I fling open the door of Cai's office, Harlen's office now. I've run straight to Harlen, and it is the right thing to do.

Harlen looks up at me and pales before I even open my mouth to speak.

"Cai has...left. He has packed his room up."

Phew, I nearly said that Cai was gone. I'm glad I managed to correct myself before giving Harlen the fright of his life. Though the thought is still clear in Harlen's eyes, as it is probably in mine. Cai could be planning to leave more than the castle.

"We need to find him!" says Harlen as he jumps to his feet.

He is right. But how? Cai wouldn't have gone anywhere that Harlen would suspect. He left without saying a word. He clearly doesn't want to be found.

"He doesn't have magic anymore," says Ri.

"I know that!" I snap.

"So you will be able to track him."

I'm great at tracking spells. It was one of the services I listed when I was a freelance mage. Hurriedly, I pull my phone out of my pocket.

"What are you doing?" asks Harlen.

"Tracking spell," I mutter as I open up a map app.

Normally I need something of the missing person. Something special to them, something that belongs to them. I don't need an object for this. I belong to Cai.

His essence is as familiar to me as my own. More so, probably.

The spell works quickly and my fingers fly over the map before dropping a pin on a small road only a few miles from here. He must have left on foot. I look up at Harlen and nod. Together we race out to his car and jump in. I pop my phone onto the holder on the dash and switch the directions on.

We drive in silence. I don't think I'm even breathing. It takes minutes, but it feels like all eternity. The road weaves around the corner and there he is. Striding along with a large rucksack on his back. He freezes. He has heard the engine, and he knows it is us.

Harlen pulls up behind him. It's a tiny road in the middle of Wales, nothing is going to be driving along it for hours and if they do, well fuck them.

I dive out of the car and run to Cai. He turns around to face us and I have a split second to see tears rolling down his face, before I smoosh myself into his chest and wrap my arms around him as best I can with the bag on his back.

"Where you going, Brat?" says Harlen softly.

I feel Cai's shrug. "Anywhere,"

Harlen sighs. "I think you should come back with us."

"I...I can't. It hurts too much."

Being in a rider fortress, surrounded by riders and the unmistakable spicy scent of dragons? I can understand that. What about the next time the siren sounds, and he has to watch us all go without him? I squeeze him tighter.

"Here's what is going to happen," says Harlen. "You are getting in the car and we are taking you to the cottage. We won't tell anyone where you are, but you better fucking be prepared for Kirby and me to visit you whenever we can."

A long silence stretches. Eventually Cai draws in a shaky breath. "Okay," he says quietly.

Then finally, finally he wraps his arms around me and returns my embrace.

After a long moment, we silently get into the car. I sit in the back and hold Cai's hand while Harlen drives. It doesn't take long. The car turns onto a road that is barely more than a track. Another ten minutes and we are in a beautiful valley surrounded by mountains. A tiny lone grey stone cottage stands by a small river. It's beautiful.

"Is this yours?" I ask.

Cai nods.

"Benefits of being stinking rich," drawls Harlen.

The faintest of smiles curls the edges of Cai's lips. This is an old thing between them. Harlen teasing him for being from a wealthy family. The familiarity must be comforting. A sign that some things will never change.

I climb out of the car. It is lovely here. I wonder if they used to sneak off here for dirty weekends. It's not far from the castle. I wait for a wave of jealousy to hit me, but it never comes. I'm glad they had each other. Even though it didn't truly work until I came along.

Harlen types in a code into a small metal box screwed into the wall next to the door. The box opens, revealing the key. He unlocks the door and we step inside.

It's a little damp and a little dusty. I start opening windows and Harlen gets to work starting a fire in the hearth. I see out of the corner of my eye the moment he reflexively starts to use his magic, then stops and reaches for the matches instead. I wonder if Cai saw it.

Cai is sitting at the table. His rucksack by his feet and a dazed look on his face.

I check the bedroom. The bed looks good and there is clean bedding in the wardrobe, so I quickly make the bed up. As I return to the front room, Harlen walks in with an armful of chopped wood. He sets it by the fireplace and dusts his hands off.

"You got food in there?" he asks, pointing to the rucksack.

Cai nods.

I suspect he has everything he needs in that bag to survive for at least a week. And the tools to survive off the land forever. The idea of Cai being unprepared is unfathomable.

"You have everything you need?"

Cai nods again.

Harlen walks up to him and softly kisses the top of his head.

"Promise me you'll be here when I come back?" Harlen whispers softly.

Cai winces, closes his eyes and nods.

"Words, Brat." rumbles Harlen.

"I'll be here," says Cai.

Harlen turns and walks away swiftly. I see tears in his eyes as he passes me. I run up to Cai and give him another hug.

"We'll be back soon!" I promise.

And then I leave, and it feels like the worst thing in the world.

Chapter Thirty-One

I open the door to the office and Harlen looks up from the laptop screen and blinks at me. It's dark in here. The sun set and he forgot to put the lights on again. I flick the switch and he winces at the sudden onslaught of light.

"Sorry!" I say. "I've brought you dinner."

The desk is strewn with papers and open files. There is no room to place the bowl of pasta that I am holding. Cai would hate to see this and I hate that such a disingenuous thought crossed my mind. Harlen is doing his best. He really is. It's not for lack of trying.

"Thanks," Harlen says with a tired smile that doesn't reach his eyes. "Paperwork sucks dick."

"Wouldn't that be a good thing?" I tease.

He chuckles, "You're right, paperwork doesn't suck dick. Dunno why I'm wasting my time with it."

I hand him the bowl of pasta and sit down in the swivel chair across the desk from him. He lifts a forkful to his mouth, but his attention is back on the computer screen and he makes no reaction to the food whatsoever. I don't mind. I'm just glad that he is eating.

"Did you know the fucking senedd refused funding to fix the collapsed sewer under the East wall, so now the whole flipping wall is going to fall down. Cai tried the National Trust but they will only help if we allow visitors to at least part of the castle. Can you imagine that? Mundane tourists and dragons? What a terrible combination."

He takes another mouthful and I just nod. Being a sounding board is the only thing I can offer. The only way I can be of any use at all.

"And one rider's girlfriend has left him with a baby and he wants to quit, but we need all the riders we can get and the only way to unbond with a dragon is to die." He pauses suddenly and takes in a deep shuddering breath. "... or burn up all your magic," he adds, in a far quieter tone.

He places the bowl of pasta down on a pile of papers and sighs heavily. He had two whole mouthfuls. Better than nothing I suppose and an improvement on yesterday. Tomorrow I will bring him something from the scoff hall, in case it is my cooking that is the problem.

I get up and pour him a glass of water from the jug by the windowsill. He takes it from me with another automatic smile. He takes a sip and places it by the pasta. It looks awfully precarious, but part of me wants all the paperwork to get destroyed. So I say nothing.

"Senedd are nagging me to get Je to choose a new rider. It's only been a fucking week. Assholes."

Harlen runs his hands through his hair. "I have no idea how Cai dealt with all of this."

"Anything I can help with?" I ask. Like I've asked before. Apparently it would take longer to teach me than to muddle through by himself, and the flight commander isn't supposed to delegate.

He shakes his head wearily. Just like I knew he would.

Time to change the subject.

"Is Je going to choose a new rider?" The very thought makes me sick to the stomach.

"Zh reckons he won't. Je and Cai were really close. Closer than most riders and dragons. Zh is worried Je is going to pine forever."

I swallow dryly. "What do they do when we die?" It's a question I have been putting off for a while now.

"Grieve for a hundred years," Harlen says solemnly.

"Oh, Ri!" I gasp.

"You are young, it's not a problem for now." replies Ri as if it is no big deal. Maybe it is the only way he can handle it.

For fuck's sake. If Cai hadn't sacrificed everything to save me. Ri would have suffered. And he might be carrying eggs. The trauma would have surely been a disaster. It is so unfair that one broken saddle girth can cause so much horror and pain.

"Oh, and we are having a party."

"What the fuck are we celebrating!" I snap, and Harlen snort laughs.

"Nothing, but riders from other castles want to meet you."

I stare at him in absolute horror but it's clear he isn't playing some sick joke on me. His dark eyes are deadly serious. I can see he is no more into this idea than I am. So clearly his hands are tied. There is going to be no escaping this. I groan in dismay.

"I'm not the chosen one."

Harlen just holds my gaze steadily. He can't believe this bullshit, can he? He seems so grounded, so down to earth and is great at reading people. He has to have read me and seen all my flaws and insecurities.

"Come on Harlen, would the chosen one suck your dick?"

He grins, a huge shit-eating grin. "Don't see why not. It's a pretty spectacular dick."

I laugh. A full belly laugh. The bastard. Everything has gone to shit, and he is making me laugh.

"Cai thinks I am," I say.

Shit. Where did that come from? I wasn't going to mention it ever, to anyone. I was going to let it fester in my soul for all eternity.

"Cai's an optimistic bastard who believes passionately in the Dragonrider cause."

I smile ruefully. "Do you think he was horrified when he realised he had been fucking the chosen one."

Harlen winks. "Not at all. He knows better than most that what a person likes between the sheets has no bearing on their ability to be a leader."

I stare at him in disbelief. "No, he doesn't! And that's his whole fucking problem!"

Harlen laughs. Deep and hearty. It reaches his eyes and I grin back at him.

"True, true. You know him well," he says eventually as he wipes tears from his eyes. "We'll get him there in the end. He will learn it's true."

Except Cai no longer needs to know that. He is not a flight commander anymore. He is a leader of nothing. All because of me.

"Not sure he will ever talk to me again once he realises that I'm not the chosen one," I say glumly. The words burn as they pass my lips but it feels damn good to get them off of my chest.

Harlen cocks his head to the side and gives me a puzzled glance. A heartbeat later, he is around the desk and picking me off the chair and into a bear hug.

"You daft fucking idiot!" he growls.

Even if he wasn't squeezing me so tight that I couldn't breathe, I still wouldn't know what to say. But despite all my bewilderment and inability to breathe, it feels wonderful to be in his arms. I want to melt and stay here forever, where he can keep me safe and make everything better.

"Cai didn't save you because he thinks you are the chosen one!" he says as he shakes me.

"Do you really think he wouldn't do the same for me, or any of the riders? You know Cai! You know he has the biggest heart of anyone alive. Or you damn well should do!"

He puts me down and I feel a little dizzy from all the shaking. His hands go to my shoulders and he stares deep into my eyes. I hold his gaze and the anger I see in him burns me with shame.

"You do know he loves you, right? You. Kirby Taylor. Not the chosen one."

My heart flutters and my eyes water. I can't breathe and this time it's not because Harlen is compressing my lungs. It's because Cai loves me.

Chapter Thirty-Two

I wouldn't call this a party, I'd call it a rave. Dragonriders are crazy motherfuckers. The main hall has been turned into a nightclub, complete with UV lighting and weird decorations, such as white netting and bits of mannequins. Rowan is rocking the DJ booth and her electric blue hair looks incredible.

About twenty riders and rider-kin are already on the dance floor even though it is still early. I watch them twist and contort their bodies to the rhythm of the music. It does kind of look fun. Almost freeing.

But I'd rather be anywhere else. Like at the cottage with Cai. Harlen and I were finally able to sneak off and see him yesterday, under the pretence of going to buy supplies for the party.

Cai doesn't want anyone else to know where he is, and I respect that. It just makes visiting him damn hard. And I don't even want to be visiting in the first place. I want us all to be living together. I want to go to sleep with him there and I want to wake up with him still there. Most of all I don't want him to be all alone in the middle of nowhere. Grieving and lost.

There is not even any phone signal in the arse end of Wales in a deep valley. What if he has an accident or something? Even though the thought of the outrageously graceful Cai doing anything like being clumsy with an axe while chopping wood, is ludicrous, it does still worry me.

Despondently, I turn and head to the kitchen. I need another drink. I only came into the hall because I hoped the music would be too loud for people to try to talk to me, and it is. But I'm not a party person at all and the music is just too loud. It's hurting my ears. Guess I was born old. And that's fine by me, I'm not ashamed of it.

The kitchen is crammed full of people. Most of them riders from other castles. I try not looking at anyone as I pour myself another drink. I need to try to find Harlen again, last time I saw him he was in the middle of a swarm of important looking people. He could probably do with backup and then he could back me up in return.

"I'm Flight Commander Henderson, pleased to meet you."

I stare at the offered hand as if it is a venomous snake. Reluctantly I shake it. It belongs to a stocky man in his early thirties, with short dark hair and dark eyes that are utterly unreadable.

"Hi," I say.

There is no point introducing myself, they all know who I am. And what would I say, anyway? 'Hi, I'm Kirby Taylor, new Dragonrider and potential chosen one.'

Henderson's dark eyes rake me over, scrutinising every inch of me. I shiver under the perlustration. There is nothing sexual in it, at least I bloody well hope not. It's all just an assessment. Trying to discern if I'm worthy.

"Can we talk?" he asks.

I thought that was what we were doing, I think snidely, but I lead him out to an empty hallway. I lean my back against the wall and try to act nonchalant.

"I've heard impressive things about you."

I shrug. I don't want this. Whatever this is. He is either about to swear fealty to me or denounce me as a fraud. Both are hideous.

His dark eyes narrow. "The senedd are tyrants. Rider numbers are falling at an alarming rate. There haven't been any dragon young for a hundred years. Now would be a great time for the Ddewiswyd to be reborn."

I stare back at him. The bass of the music is thrumming through the wall behind me. Giving the castle a heartbeat.

"People need hope. Something to believe."

A shiver dances along my spine. So this is where this is going. He has come to the same conclusion that I have. If enough people believe that I am the chosen one, then it makes it true. Reality is irrelevant. It's faith that turns the wheel.

"They can believe in someone else," I say tonelessly.

Something flashes across his eyes. "They have already chosen you, can't you feel it?"

"They can unchoose me and choose you instead!" I snap.

"You are new, young, good-looking, powerful. You fit the bill, whether you like it or not."

I glare at him. Despite the magnitude of the situation, I'm still horribly flustered at being called good-looking. Unusual looking I can accept, a guy with waist length red hair is not something you see every day, but it makes me uncomfortable to think that people don't see the same thing that I do when I look in the mirror.

"You're already paying the price for it, so why not take some of the glory?" he asks.

This guy is relentless. And what the hell is he talking about? He sees my confusion and takes in a deep breath.

"Do you really think your saddle girth snapping was an accident?"

Everything freezes. The pulse of the music pauses between beats. The beams of dim light solidify. Dust motes hold still mid air. I cease breathing. My heart stills. My blood becomes darkness. I can feel the void and it is laughing.

Someone had cleaned my saddle. I had noticed that. They had used a sweet smelling oil. I had liked the aroma.

I'm a naïve clueless idiot. It never crossed my mind that someone might imbue the oil with magic or an acid. Something that would eat away at the girth.

The saddle fell into the sea, and we never thought to retrieve it. It was never examined.

For a moment, I'm falling through the cold sky again. The tattered and frayed girth fluttering in the air like a pretty ribbon. I blink and I'm back in the silent and frozen hallway with Henderson, but I'm still falling. I'll always be falling now.

The senedd want to cling onto their power. Not everyone will be happy to see a chosen one return. Even a fake one. The prospect alone is enough to scare them. People were willing to murder me and they destroyed Cai instead.

Moving my body feels like wading through treacle but I keep going. I turn away from Henderson. I have no idea if he says anything as I leave.

Somehow I make it back to the apartment. I open the door to Cai's empty room and find Harlen sitting on the bare bed. Like me, he is searching for some essence of Cai, some lingering trace to hold onto. But there is nothing here. It's just a barren room.

Cai is a few miles away. All alone in a cottage.

"There is an old coal mine in the mountain behind the cottage," says Ri. *"It would only take a night to dig a dragon sized entrance to it."*

"Can they do anything to stop us taking our dragons and leaving?" I ask Harlen and my voice sounds fierce.

Harlen blinks at me in confusion. "No," he answers carefully. "But they need us. There are barely enough dragons and riders to hold back the tylwyth as it is."

I know he is right. I'm furious at riders, and I will be no one's puppet, but I'm not spiteful enough to let the world burn. I'm not deranged. I'm still going to protect my home and the countless innocent lives on Earth.

"The dragons can tell Ri and Zh if the siren sounds, and we could still fight," I tell Harlen, as I question Ri. Sabotaging or assassinating me when we only meet in air, is going to be a fucking challenge for any bastard who wants to try it.

"Yes!" answers Ri.

Harlen just stares at me. His eyes wide and dark. It is a lot for him to take in. I have sprung it on him out of nowhere.

"Well, I'm taking Ri and moving into the cottage with Cai. You can stay here and be flight commander."

"Fuck that!" exclaims Harlen as he jumps to his feet.

"Je has decided to come too. Cai can still ride, even though he can't fight."

I see a flash of gold in Harlen's eyes as presumably Zh tells him the same thing and then a huge shit-eating grin spreads across Harlen's face. My heart flutters. The first taste of happiness in weeks starts to flow within me, igniting a flame of hope.

"The look on Cai's face when we turn up with our dragons is going to be priceless," says Harlen delightedly.

I grin back at him. It is. It really, truly is going to be priceless, and I can't wait to see it.

Chapter Thirty-Three

Stretching out in the bed is glorious. It really is too small for three grown men to share, so now that the others have got up and started their days, it's nice to unfurl my limbs. The late summer sun feels wonderful on my naked skin. If I open my eyes, I know the small window will give me a splendid view of the green valley.

I love it here. The cottage is tiny, and we need new furniture, but I wouldn't change it for the world. There is no phone signal, no internet, no television. It's like stepping back in time. And obviously, best of all, Cai and Harlen are here with me.

A floorboard creaks and I open one eye. Cai is standing in the doorway, wet from his shower and wearing only a tiny towel around his waist. It's a fantastic view. Far better than looking at the valley. All that gleaming wet naked chest, yummy. I could stare at it for days.

Cai is staring at me too. Oh. Oops. I'm sprawled naked on the bed with my morning wood on full display. I hold my breath and fight my urge to cover myself up.

Slow minutes tick by as Cai's gaze slowly makes its way over my body and up to my face. He looks at me and there is fire in his summer storm coloured eyes.

"Get on your knees and open your mouth," he rasps, gesturing at the floor in front of him.

My heart races, and my stomach flips over. I nearly fall out of bed in my enthusiasm to get to him. Talk about best breakfast ever.

A shiver of excitement raises the small hairs on my arms. I want to taste Cai on my tongue, with a yearning so strong it hurts, but most of all, I'm thrilled his sex drive is returning. Harlen and I have been here a week, and it's just been kisses and cuddles. Cai getting his mojo back is wonderful, not just because I'm a horny fiend, but because it means he is healing.

I drop to my knees and open my mouth obediently. The towel drops to the floor with a dull thud. The moan that comes out of me as Cai feeds me his hard cock, is utterly depraved and carnal sounding. I'm not embarrassed. Not in the slightest. Once I would have been mortified. Not anymore. There is no shame in making love. None at all.

The weight of Cai on my tongue is bliss. I lather his cock with affection. He tastes good, damn good. His breath hitches a little and his long slender fingers card through my hair to caress my scalp. He guides me gently with his touch and I surrender to his command.

"Guys, have you seen my…" Harlen says as he walks into the bedroom. His footsteps freeze. "Don't stop," he rumbles.

"Wasn't going to!" snaps Cai.

I just keep diligently working away. Not getting involved is definitely the best thing to do when they are bickering.

"Do you know what would make Kirby's luscious lips rolling over your cock feel even better? Me in your ass."

"No!" says Cai, while my cock twitches. The image is great, and the praise is hot. I definitely have a growing praise kink.

"Fuck Kirby instead," Cai gasps.

I whimper.

"Okay," drawls Harlen and the promise twists in my guts. "But first I'm going to help make you scream. There is no one out here, Brat. So you can let go."

Harlen's soft footsteps come closer. My eyes open and I look up. Harlen is standing behind Cai, nuzzling his neck. Tanned fingers are toying with Cai's pale pink nipples. Cai's head falls back to loll on Harlen's shoulder and Harlen grins.

"So sensitive," he whispers into Cai's ear. "One day, I'm going to lie you on the bed, tie your arms above your head and give Kirby one nipple and I will take the other. We will suck, lick and flick and see if we can make you cum."

Cai's cock throbs in my mouth and he moans softly.

"It might take hours, but you will writhe and buck and swear at us so beautifully. Our hands will trace along your body, teasing and caressing but never touching your cock or ass."

The noise Cai makes can only be described as a whimper. My cock leaks. Fucking hell, Harlen is painting a hot image. I want to do it now.

Cai's nipples are hard nubs now and the way Harlen's clever fingers are dancing over them, makes me moan. I want his hands on me like that. I move my own hand to one of my tingling nipples but it's not the same.

"Then, when you are sobbing and begging for mercy, I'll take one of Kirby's fingers and slide it into your ass with one of mine and teach him all the right ways to stroke you."

Cai's cock pulses and for a moment I think he has cum, but it's just a burst of pre-cum. He is not far off though. His legs are trembling and his breathing is shaky and rapid.

"And after hours of being tormented and edged, we will watch you cum and you will scream so beautifully for us. Your back will arch and you will be completely undone. Then, while you are trying to remember how to breathe, I'll give you my cock."

Cai's groan is so deep I feel it in my chest. I pick up the pace of my slide up and down his cock.

"Kirby!"

"Kind of busy right now, Ri!"

"Kirby! Kirby!"

"What?"

"I felt my eggs quicken! I'm going to lay eggs that might hatch!"

Ri's pride and excitement is so strong that it almost feels like a solid thing that can be touched. I can see him turning around and around, like an excited puppy, in his new burrow in the old coal mine. He hasn't told Je and Zh yet, and I'm beyond flattered that I'm the first person he shared his news with.

I pull off of Cai's cock and stare up at my lovers.

"Ri's eggs have quickened!" I gasp breathlessly. I need to get better at remembering to breathe while sucking cock.

Cai lifts his head from Harlen's shoulder, as his eyes snap open. The sapphire depths are dark and hazy with lust, but he smiles, a great beaming smile of joy and happiness.

Harlen grins, and his dark eyes flash with glee. "Look at you, my little Khaleesi, mother of dragons."

I roll my eyes at him. "Don't call me that."

He chuckles evilly as he tilts his head at Cai's hard and glistening cock, which is bobbing in front of my face.

"You've got a job to finish, Khaleesi."

I glare at him, but lean forward and take Cai's wet cock back into my mouth. The noise Cai makes tells me this job is not going to take too long to finish.

"That's it Khaleesi, press your tongue against his slit and get ready to swallow."

Why do I get the feeling Harlen is going to call me that from now on? And why on earth am I going to like it?

Cai cries out and thrusts into my mouth, ropes of cum spill down my throat as his entire body spasms. His orgasm rolls on and on, and I'm pleased and proud, as well as jealous.

I release his cock and Cai sags bonelessly in Harlen's arms, while breathing heavily. Harlen half carries, half drags him over to the dilapidated armchair in the corner, then he comes and stands before me with an enormous bulge in his grey sweatpants.

"Get on the bed for your turn, Khaleesi."

I make a noise that is supposed to be a protest, but I don't think I'm fooling anyone. I can't stop grinning as I climb onto the bed.

I love my life.

What happens next?

Will Ri's eggs hatch?
Will the senedd leave our boys alone?
Can Kirby really walk away so easily?
Are the tylwyth really the bad guys?

If people enjoy DragonRider, these questions and more will be answered in DragonSeer, in Harlen's point of view and DragonKing, in Cai's point of view.

So please rate, review or recommend DragonRider!

For now, please see the next page for how to get one more chapter of Kirby, Harlen & Cai

Thank You for reading DragonRider

Want more Kirby, Cai & Harlen?
How about a FREE exclusive bonus epilogue?

Tap the link to sign up to my monthly newsletter for instant access!

https://www.srodman.net/newsletter-sign-up.html

If you are already a subscriber, don't worry! The link was in the 23rd June 2023 newsletter.
(If you signed up after that date, follow the link in your welcome email.)

Limited time offer **Not one, but TWO free books when you sign up!**
Sign up now and your welcome email will contain links not only for the bonus epilogue but also for a free copy of Incubus Broken and Omega Alone.

If none of that takes your fancy, how about exclusive short stories and opportunities to receive free copies of new books before they are released?

Sign up here.

https://www.srodman.net/newsletter-sign-up.html

It comes out once a month, you can unsubscribe at any time and I never spam, because we all hate spam.

If the link is broken please scan the QR code below or type www.srodman.net into your brower.

Books By S. Rodman

For an up to date list, you can view my Amazon Author page HERE
Or view at www.srodman.net

Darkstar Pack

Evil Omega

Evilest Omega

Evil Overlord Omega

Duty & Magic: MM Modern Day Regency

Lord Garrington's Vessel

Earl Hathbury's Vessel

The Bodyguard's Vessel

Duke Sothbridge's Vessel

Found & Freed: The Unfettered

Unfettered Omega

Non Series

DragonRider

All Rail the King

Shipped: A Hollywood Gay Romance

Hunted By The Omega

Hell Broken

Past Life Lover

How to Romance an Incubus

Lost & Loved

Dark Mage Chained

Prison Mated

Incubus Broken

Omega Alone

Printed in Great Britain
by Amazon